If I Knew
I'd Tell You

OTHER BOOKS BY CAROL MALYON

Headstand
The Edge of the World
Emma's Dead

If I Knew I'd Tell You

A NOVEL BY

CAROL MALYON

The Mercury Press

§

i need to thank a lot of people

this was written in donut shops & other people's homes. thanks to
jane and john for bellefair ave, richard and ann for middleton, libby
for queen's quay, helen for sussex ave, bill for richmond st

thanks to everyone who read it first: kristin andrychuk, thea caplan,
john dodge, bill howell, helen humphreys, jane malyon, john
macneill, ted plantos. thanks to bev & don daurio who somehow find
time to publish other people's books

thanks to the ontario arts council

§

The publisher gratefully acknowledges the financial assistance
of the Canada Council, the Ontario Arts Council, and of the
Government of Ontario through the Ontario Publishing Centre.

Edited by Beverley Daurio
Cover design by Gordon Robertson
Printed and bound in Canada by Coach House Printing
Printed on acid-free paper

First Printing, September 1993
1 2 3 4 5 97 96 95 94 93

CANADIAN CATALOGUING IN PUBLICATION DATA:
Malyon, Carol, 1933-
If I knew I'd tell you
ISBN 1-55128-003-5
I. Title.
PS8576.A536415 1993   C813'.54   C93-094760-6
PR9199.3.M34I5 1993

Represented in Canada by the Literary Press Group
Distributed by General Publishing

The Mercury Press
137 Birmingham Street
Stratford, Ontario
Canada N5A 2T1

we time-share the world

for
bill bissett
&
helen humphreys

Uneasily the leaves fall at this season,
forgetting what to do or where to go;
the red amnesiacs of autumn
drifting thru the graveyard forest.

What they have forgotten they have forgotten:
what they meant to do instead of fall
is not in earth or time recoverable—
the fossils of intention, the shapes of rot.

— Al Purdy

SUSAN

There is something in the attic. Susan is beginning to believe this.

But it is hearsay; she has never heard the sounds herself. It is also inaccurate; there is no attic. But it doesn't matter. Susan's daughter hears noises up there anyway, in the place where an attic would be, if they had one. Each night Angela hears noises above her bedroom ceiling & is frightened.

Susan tells her, *Stop being silly. There's nothing up there. You must be dreaming.*

Anyway, there is no attic. They both know this.

No dusty room of ancestral treasures, no old treadle sewing machine, dressmaker's dummy, great-grandmother's bisque dolls, no wardrobe trunk of old clothes to dress up in at Hallowe'en. No trapdoor in the ceiling where Susan could climb a ladder & peer inside, looking for creatures who make sounds. If she was brave enough to do this. It is debatable whether Susan would be brave enough or not. She's glad she doesn't have to find out.

Angela is 16 now, & strong & beautiful. She certainly is brave enough, but Susan wouldn't want her to climb up & look, considering it to be one of those dangerous undertakings which she, being the mother, should take care of herself. How long will she continue to feel this way? they both wonder, as

Angela grows older & more capable, as Susan grows older, & less.

Fortunately for Susan, it doesn't matter. She doesn't have to climb up there. There is no way to see inside the space beneath the roof.

There is something in the attic. Now Susan says this to teachers she works with, to anyone who'll pay attention. Soon she'll tell strangers on the subway. She'd tell her friends if she still saw them.

I've a ghost in the attic, she says, & laughs. *The Ghost in the Attic. It sounds like a title for a B-movie.* She says this, even though she has no attic. She doesn't really have the house; she moved in only two months ago & still feels like an intruder. The creature making noises preceded her, & may still be here after she's gone.

There is something in the attic, she keeps saying. You can believe her if you want to. Not everyone does.

There is no space for a proper attic, but there are gaps between the bedroom ceiling & the roof. There must be; the ceiling is flat but the roof above is slanted. Also there are spaces behind the walls, & gaps between the walls & floors; so many places in the house where Susan can lie down on the floor & peer behind the walls. She is looking for something alive, but sees nothing, hears nothing. The house is silent. *Not a mouse stirring,* as the soldier reports in *Hamlet; not a creature is stirring,* as on the night before Christmas.

Susan is aware of empty spaces everywhere, gaps in her life, years she can't remember. Chunks of memory are missing. Where could they have gone?

She tests herself. *How about the year Angela was seven years old?* she wonders. *How much can you remember?* She talks aloud to make sure she pays attention.

Angela would have been in grade two. Susan can't remember that grade at all. The year existed; otherwise Angela couldn't have moved on to grade three. Susan studies a school picture from the year she thinks must be grade two. A child resembling Angela sits in the front row. She wears clothes Susan remembers, but of course, she could be remembering them from grade one or grade three.

Susan is 44 years old. Thousands of memories should be jumbled inside her mind & tumble out when she wakens every morning. Instead: one memory, over & over, blocking the others out, the way white noise muffles other sounds.

Susan worries about these memory lapses. Things must have happened: world affairs & family ones. But maybe not. Perhaps the year consisted only of going to work & coming home, washing one load of laundry after another, 365 poached egg breakfasts, peanut butter & jam lunches in brown paper bags, 365 different ways to cook ground beef for supper. A thousand meals. She had a husband then. *How was your day?* she would have asked him; *How was yours?* he'd have asked back. They were always polite.

She could ask old friends about the year Angela was seven. *Was I strange then?* Susan could ask them, but won't, afraid they won't know what she's talking about, even more afraid they might. She doesn't see her old friends anyway. They came in couples. She has shed them like worn-out clothes.

She is missing the year her daughter was in grade two, & other years as well. New acquaintances don't seem to notice. Susan looks the same age as they are. They assume her years were full of experiences she remembers. Susan pretends this is true.

Is this what happens as we get older? she wonders. Is there a finite amount of memory available? New things happen & crowd old memories out, like an overloaded circuit, a fire in a warehouse. Old files fed into a paper shredder. An erase button pushed on a computer. So many memories not worth saving anyway. Garbage in, garbage out: GIGO. But Susan would like to decide for herself which memories to delete.

She will have to write down the good ones & store them in steel boxes. She tries to remember some:

A man & woman are young & beautiful & shine with health. They run along a beach of packed white sand. He is tanned & muscular & strong enough to hold her. She is radiant & independent & looks like she wouldn't let him. He picks her up anyway. She flings her arms around his neck. Seagulls squawk to each other inside their sky for reassurance. The man & woman hold each other tight & assume nothing will ever change. People watch them. The couple knows this but doesn't care. Other people have never been in love.

She can see it clearly, like the cover of a romance novel on a revolving rack inside a drug store.

Should she keep this memory? She can't decide.

Or:

A baby is born. It forces its way down through the mother, emerges between her legs, splits the mother's body like a peach. The baby emerges into cold dry air, bright lights that hurt its eyes. It screams with shock. The umbilical cord is cut. Now the baby has to keep breathing or else die. The mother cradles the infant in her warm arms, places a nipple between its lips. Milk is created inside the mother's body when she does this.

This memory is a 'keeper.' There must be others, but she can't find them. They are like children in Chile who are missing without a trace or explanation.

She was married for more than 20 years. If her husband was here he could say, *Remember...* & mention something that happened & suddenly Susan would remember it too. *Remember the year Angela was seven?* she could ask, & wait to see what he said. *Wasn't that the year we took the kids for a picnic in the park for her birthday & it rained?* he could reply. She'd say, *No. It didn't rain. It teamed buckets. It was a deluge. It's a wonder we didn't drown. Imagine the headlines if we had: 'Birthday Party Drowned Out.'* He'd disagree. *They don't pun in headlines,* he'd say. *They don't intentionally,* she'd answer. *This one slipped by.*

If he was here alive beside her perhaps they'd be able to talk like this. She thinks they used to.

Susan has read about shock therapy. Doctors strap a patient down & zap the head. Whole blocks of memory disintegrate. Perhaps this happened & she doesn't remember it, because of course the memory of having electric shock would have disintegrated too.

Meanwhile: this year; Angela; noises in an imaginary attic.

Susan intends to forget this year as soon as possible, but not yet. Too much is happening. There is action above her daughter's ceiling. Angela hears it. Perhaps Susan will do something about it. Maybe she will call someone tomorrow, if she can think of some appropriate person.

Susan lives inside this house with her 16-year-old daughter & a photograph album, black & white reminders of a husband fastened neatly inside: a man stands beside Susan, his arm around her shoulder; he stands beside Angela, his hand resting on her head; he sits on the porch with a cat on his lap. There is no snapshot to show him inside the car that killed him.

Susan hides inside the house with Angela & a cat & glossy memories of a dead husband. This is all she can cope with. She thinks it's unfair to have to deal with more. She can't handle the existence of a creature in a non-existent attic.

She prepares for classes, marks school papers; she hides in libraries, shrouded by books.

Angela is always hopeful. She tries to believe Susan will do something. She pretends she doesn't notice how Susan avoids decisions, how her pale eyes find excuses to wander away from problems right in front, how she chews on her fingernails whenever Angela mentions the noises.

Angela is able to pretend because she has had lots of practice. Perhaps she can make herself believe that when Susan says, *Leave me a note on the fridge to remind me, so I'll do something about it in the morning,* Susan really will. Susan certainly intends to.

But Susan DID move to this house two months ago; she left her old life behind her, a couple of dozen blocks away. She stayed in the same district so Angela would be close to her friends, but she didn't need to; Angela spends all her spare time with her grandparents anyway.

Now Susan wishes she'd moved farther away. But it's too late. All her courage has been used up. She waits for more to accumulate inside her, like red blood cells after a haemorrhage.

This house has no driveway or garage. Susan never intends to climb inside a car again.

Self-stick paper was invented with Susan & Angela in mind. Each time the refrigerator door is opened, pages flutter like yellow butterflies.

Notes from Susan:

I can't find my red sweater.

Where are my new sunglasses? Put them back.

Don't forget to put out the garbage before you leave for school.

There's a tuna casserole in the fridge. Put it in the oven at 5 o'clock.

Notes from Angela:

The noises woke me up again last night.

The cat threw up on the hall rug. I'll clean it later.

The TV won't work.

Don't buy the cat Krunchies. He hates them.

Something is alive above my ceiling. Do something!

SUSAN

Saturdays & Sundays Susan relaxes; she can do whatever she wants. No one nags her about noises. Angela visits her grandparents every weekend. What do they talk about? Susan wonders, but she knows: Angela talks about her father, the grandparents talk about their son.

So many hours. 48! Susan can't imagine what to do.

Saturday morning she does the laundry: two hours. She cleans the house: another hour, but not really, because she vacuums while the clothes are in the dryer. Then Susan goes out to buy groceries & doesn't come back.

She sits in Civilizations where they make great coffee. This is what their ad says, & it's true.

She has decided to make this restaurant the setting for her novel. It is time to stop taking notes, time to start writing & do something with her life. She has 48 hours every weekend & can't use lack of time as an excuse any longer. A dresser drawer is stuffed with scraps of paper, serviettes, notes scribbled in donut shops & on streetcars. Indecipherable bits of dialogue & description, plot outlines.

Now Susan keeps a notebook inside her purse, so she always has it handy.

She has taken creative writing courses. *Write what you know,* they advise. *Keep it authentic.*

Last week she found a typewriter at a garage sale. Carrying

it home, she wondered, do people think I look like a real writer? She looked at her store-window reflection & almost thought so herself.

As though there are layers of her own life she knows nothing about.

When she began to type up her notes she discovered the lower case b was broken off, & had to use the capital instead. Gradually she is getting used to this & likes it. She thinks it helps establish a wonky style. Is it symbolic of something? she wonders.

The woman sits alone at a kitchen taBle every weekend. She fills in crossword puzzles, reads newspapers & liBrary Books from the recommended shelf. She clips out recipes she knows she'll never try & copies them into a Binder. She prints fresh laBels for spice rack Bottles. She sorts out snapshots & fastens them in an alBum. She knows it would Be Better if her activities involved people, But has only enough energy for what she's doing.

Now Susan sits in Civilizations, her notebook open, her pencil lined up neatly beside it, & she waits for inspiration. Finally she starts to write in neat school-teacher script:

The woman sits in a restaurant drinking coffee. The table-top is made of something synthetic, Formica maybe, with a matte finish. It sprouts like a blossom on top of a dark green pedestal base...

No, Susan thinks, too flowery. Then she thinks, pun.

The woman sits at a table in the restaurant, her feet twined like ivy around the dark green pedestal base...

Better.

Susan concentrates on her novel, forgets her house, the notes fastened to the fridge: *Do something.*

She sips her coffee, & studies the empty chair across from her. The scrolls of beige wood, curved like cane or wicker. How do they bend the wood without it breaking? she wonders. She imagines an artisan. His hands are strong yet gentle. He soaks the wood in boiling water until it's supple, then slowly curves it into shape. His brow is furrowed in concentration. Each time he creates a perfect pattern he allows himself to smile.

Each chair is slightly different. Susan presses her back against the curved wood & concentrates on feeling the pattern with her skin. Hundreds of people have sat upon this chair, & felt this pattern against their backs. Probably they didn't even notice. But the memory of the pattern is still imprinted beneath their skin. Susan has something in common with them. Even now, similar patterns indent the backs of all the people in this restaurant, like the heroine of her novel, whatever the heroine's name is, whatever the name of the novel is. The heroine sits on this chair at this table & watches whatever happens.

The woman feels the cane pattern of the chair pressing against her. An archaeologist could rub chalk against the back of her blouse & trace the imprint. Inside old cathedrals smelling of damp & history, people rub brasses, trying to sort out the past & understand things. The woman would like to understand things herself.

Or, the heroine will work here. That might be better. She will speak to all the customers, & smile at the regulars like Susan. The heroine will know the other people on staff & learn their stories.

A girl stands behind the cash register. Her long blonde hair is twisted into a braid. Someone calls to her from the kitchen, *Hey, Cassie.* Susan tries writing the name down; it looks good upon the page. She says *Cassie* quietly; it feels good against her tongue. She decides to borrow it for her story.

There is a busboy Cassie keeps watching. No one notices this except Susan. Perhaps Cassie assumes a quiet woman with a pencil won't tell anyone, that writers keep secrets. Cassie has probably never known a writer before.

It is hot. Ceiling fans turn round & round, giving an illusion of coolness. Susan thinks of southern mansions. Pale delicate women sprawl on *chaises longues.* They sip mint juleps. Ice clinks. Moisture forms a silver mist on the outside of each glass. The women trace patterns in the moisture with slender manicured fingers. They flutter their silk fans, gracefully, knowing exactly how to do this. They learned as children. Their southern accents are flawless. In the shadows Tennessee Williams watches them. He writes everything down.

Susan wants to do this with Civilizations. Immortalize it. Report it authentically.

She would like to do this with her daughter too. Perhaps she could pretend Angela works here. Writing about her daughter would be a way to become close to her again. All the action in the novel would have to take place on weekdays after school, because Angela visits her grandparents every weekend. That's as close to her dead father as she can get, & takes her far away from whatever makes a racket above her ceiling.

Whenever Angela mentions her father Susan changes the subject to something else.

What did the person in the kitchen call the cashier? Susan wonders. Oh yes. Cassie. Susan will pretend that Angela works here & is named Cassie. Angela couldn't be a cashier though; her math is terrible. She will have to work behind the counter serving out food.

Cassie is 16. She works at Civilizations after school to avoid ghosts.

Her mother permits it. Cassie is brave & needs to try things. She is different from her mother. They both know this.

It began when Cassie's father was still alive.

Cassie loved him best, hung around him, ran to meet him when he came home from work.

Her mother thought this was cute.

Her father was flattered, of course; he began paying more attention to his daughter than his wife.

Her mother didn't mind; perhaps she even preferred it. She & her husband had run out of things to talk about. This isn't something she'd admit. Not to her daughter or anyone.

Cassie plans to marry a man just like her father but she'll never end up like her mother. A husband dies; a wife breaks into little pieces.

Cassie is the strong one in the family now. She refuses to look after her mother. She'll have to do so soon enough.

She has made a start! Susan looks at her neat words on the pages & can hardly believe it.

SUSAN & ANGELA

Angela comes home each Sunday evening & looks hopeful. *I didn't do anything about the noises*, Susan tells her.

CASSIE

Cassie stands at the cash desk & looks around the room. She can look anywhere she wants because her father hasn't come in yet.

People sit at tables. They eat, drink coffee, have quiet conversations, read newspapers or books.

A woman writes in a notebook, her cup of coffee untouched beside her. What is she writing? Cassie wonders. She has seen this woman somewhere else.

SUSAN

Susan dawdles over her coffee in Civilizations, but eventually has to return home.

She walks slowly, but gets there anyway.

She has only lived here two months, but can hardly remember the previous place. What was her life like there? she wonders. She has snapshots in an album, & can look at them if she needs to know.

She has never lived in a place like this before. In other houses the walls come all the way down to meet the floors. Baseboards & quarter-round fasten the walls & floors together.

In this house, Susan's new *old* house, walls dangle from the ceiling, but don't reach down far enough. The baseboard & quarter-round are gone. There are spaces between the walls & floors.

A neighbour tells her a story: One winter the landlord stopped paying utility bills. After the gas was turned off, tenants pried off loose pieces of woodwork & burned them in the fireplace in order to keep warm. Perhaps this is true, perhaps not, it doesn't matter, but pieces of wood *are* missing. Sections of moulding gone from doorways & windows. Their ghostly outlines remain, creating pale albino patterns on painted walls. Susan notices the absence of stain around the edge of the hardwood floors.

Susan is aware of these absences more & more as time goes

on. When she moved in she hardly noticed anything missing; now everywhere she looks she is startled by another absence of wood. As though she stares at a jigsaw puzzle someone else has fitted together; it is old & some of the pieces have been lost; at first Susan saw only the pretty scene & didn't notice random blank sections. Now it seems more & more pieces are missing, as though every time she glances away another one is removed.

Some creature leaves the attic, scurries down behind the wall, emerges through the gap between the wall & floor, foraging for loose bits of wood. It must seem like a game to it, Susan thinks. How long before she notices a section of plate rail is missing? The moulding by the front door? The baseboard on the landing? The trim above her bedroom window?

The walls hang there. They wait for something to rest on or fasten to. They remind Susan of acrobats who've been abandoned. An acrobat dangles from a trapeze. The person he was supposed to swing to is missing. The circus is over; the audience has gone home but the acrobat still hangs there. He will dangle there forever unless someone does something about it. It is debatable whether anyone will. Susan lies awake at night & imagines acrobats are swinging. They are exhausted. She hears them weakly call for help.

Sometimes she lies down on the floor & peers into the gap where the baseboard ought to be. The walls stop an inch above the floor, or rather, they stop an inch above where the floor would be if the floor went far enough, if the floor didn't also stop an inch too short. Anything could hide behind those walls & watch her.

Mice could scamper down behind the plaster & enter all the rooms. There is nothing to stop them. Susan feels their beady eyes watch her; their pink noses quiver; their whiskers are fine-tuned toward her like sensitive antennae.

Sometimes she shouts into a crevice, *Come out, come out, wherever you are,* an old chant from childhood hide & seek games. If they keep hiding, someone will have to go in there & find them. Perhaps she will meet a man from Hamelin who'll pipe them out. Not that she wants to meet a man, of course not, but if she did he would probably know what to do.

Susan lies down on the floor looking for mice, calling to them, but only on weekends when Angela is not at home. *Don't be scared,* Susan tells them. *No one else is here. I'm all alone.* But they don't come out to see her. The mice don't answer. Nothing does.

She could buy mouse-traps & learn how to set them. She remembers a quote from Saki:

> *In baiting a mouse-trap with cheese, always leave room for the mouse.*

She could buy mouse-traps, but is afraid to. The cheese might tempt the mice out into the open. Anyway, Susan is not into assassination. She's into writing.

Angela is visiting her grandparents again. It is time for Susan to drink coffee at Civilizations & work on her story.

Cassie lives with her mother in an old house in an old neighbourhood full of shade trees. The leaves are starting to fall now, & beyond them other houses gradually appear. Each morning when Cassie looks out her bedroom window, the houses are a little clearer, as though someone fills in their missing pieces while she sleeps.

Each day Cassie arrives at school exhausted from listening to noises above her bed all night. *There's nothing up there,* her mother tells her. *How could there be?*

She must be right. How could there? Cassie wonders this too. How could some creature get in & out?

Cassie doesn't think she still believes in ghosts. Old stories told around campfires, while noises rustle in the bush...

Maybe someone died here, she tells her mother. *Maybe a ghost is looking for a way out.*

Don't be silly, says her mother, because that's the way that mothers talk.

Susan thinks about mice. Surely her cat would catch them.

SUSAN

Susan looks around her world & notices there are no men left.

The ones her age play old ideas in their minds, like dance song lines that keep repeating on worn-out 78s. Their words are plagiarized from Humphrey Bogart movies & Archie comic books. They hum along to Mantovani & Muzak.

Anyway, they fantasize about her daughter. Susan wants to sleep with their sons.

SUSAN

Susan alliterates today: 44, 44, 44. She thinks there's nothing good to say about it, except it's better than 55 or 66 or 77.

44. Susan says it over & over, noticing how the sound links 40 & four together, like a marriage between acquaintances. They like each other at 22 & hope that it's enough.

This 44-year-old woman though, this intruder in her kitchen, who scrambles eggs & reads the morning paper: perhaps she looks for an article to explain who they both are, these women, the one who's 44, & the one who pretends she's still 33 & can choose whichever alliteration she wishes.

Perhaps she'll tell someone at work it's her birthday. *44! I can't believe it. Because I still pretend I'm 10 years younger.* Then she'll laugh, because it's okay to say it if you laugh.

Wishing it was funny. Every morning she sees an acquaintance in the mirror. Not a stranger, but not her.

For supper they order pizza. Angela sits Susan down in front of the TV to watch an *I Love Lucy* re-run. *Get comfortable,* she says. *I'll bring in the pizza.*

She seems to take forever. Finally a blaze of light. 44 candles drip coloured wax onto anchovies & pepperoni. Angela has to peel the wax off. Susan can't see to do it because she's crying.

CASSIE

Cassie likes working at Civilizations. People slide their trays toward her & trust her to know what each thing costs. Cassie pushes cash register keys & enjoys the ringing sound. Sometimes she can hardly keep from tapping her feet to the cling & clang & cling. But this is a job. She has to be dignified.

The sound reminds her of pinball machines, & she wonders why. Did her father play pinball with her when he lived at home? She can't remember. Anyway, this job keeps her too busy to think... about him or anyone.

All these people, the customers, the staff: it is so easy to be pleasant to them. They don't demand anything but food. They don't require her love & forgiveness & understanding. Also, she keeps learning new things. This restaurant serves foods she's never eaten before: pine nuts, chili, caesar salad. Foods she had never even heard of: tofu, alfalfa sprouts, fettucini.

Her grandmother cooks liver & onions, stew & dumplings, shepherd's pie, like her own grandmother before her; substantial foods, solid. *They stick to your ribs,* says Cassie's grandmother. When Cassie imagines liver sticking to her ribs she feels like throwing up.

The time at work passes quickly. Always Cassie has to leave before she's ready. She saunters home daydreaming about the lives of the people she sees at Civilizations. It doesn't last though; soon she remembers people in her own life. Some of them she loves but doesn't understand.

CASSIE

Her grandmother is dozing on the porch swing when Cassie comes home from work. Cassie touches her gently on the arm.

Hiya Gran, she says. *I'm home now. You can stop waiting up for me & go to bed.*

Her grandmother squints & rubs her eyes. *Cassandra?* she asks.

I wish you'd call me Cassie like everyone else.

But it's not your name.

Cassie sighs. Her grandmother always calls her Cassandra. This is the sort of thing grandmothers do.

But a grandmother is always there. She can be counted on.

She took in her daughter & grandchild when the daughter & son-in-law split up. When her daughter moved in with someone else she kept the grandchild. She doesn't seem to take sides. She never says anything unkind about either of Cassie's parents, & keeps encouraging Cassie to see them.

They care about you, she tells Cassie. *Just go to see them. Don't shut them out. Don't try to understand them. They're just human. Nobody's perfect.*

Cassie gets mad & starts to holler so she won't cry. *Why should I bother with either of them? They're lousy parents & you know it. They both walked out on me.*

Her grandmother sighs. They've been over this before.

Cassie hugs her grandmother. *I wish they'd move to the other side of the world & leave me alone. I don't care about either of them. You're the only one I love.*

Grandmothers say words like *Cassandra, duty, honour, tradition, respect.* They're uncomfortable with that L-word: *love.*

Cassie knows her grandmother loves her even though she doesn't say it, but it doesn't seem like enough. She wonders, is it ever possible to get enough love?

DAVID & CASSIE

David doesn't have much time to see his daughter. He visits his father each evening after work. He comes into Civilizations Saturday & Sunday mornings.

Cassie wants to be a psychologist some day. Right now she reads pop psychology books every chance she gets. David thinks Cassie knows too much already. She watches TV soaps & sees right through him.

Stop visiting Grandpa all the time, says Cassie, when she's in the mood for talking to David at all. *He doesn't even know you. You just do it because it's easy.*

It's partly true, David thinks. His father IS so easy to visit. He says nothing, demands nothing, doesn't look at David with reproach. He opens his mouth when he is told to, eats whatever he's fed. They walk up & down the hall together & no words are possible between them. David is not required to speak.

SUSAN

The car crash. For months afterward Susan dreams it & wakes up shaking.

Her husband on his way back from a selling trip in northern Ontario, not expected until tomorrow. Perhaps he intends to surprise them, have coffee brewing for breakfast by the time Susan & Angela wake up, be mixing pancake batter as a special treat.

He drives along a lonesome stretch of highway in the middle of the night. Beyond the shoulder a steep hill drops toward a creek.

He is tired & dozes off. I'll just rest my eyes a moment, he thinks.

The car swerves & startles him awake. He twists the wheel. Jams on the brakes. Panic. Loud noises all around him. Small bushes rush at the windshield. Branches crack, scratch at the car; rocks thump against it. The car tumbles sideways. Overturns. Rolls over & over.

Does he have time to form coherent thoughts? Does his life roll backwards in fast motion? Does he die saying, *Susan Susan Susan*?

The car finally stops at the bottom of the ravine, gas spurts, ignites...

It doesn't matter. He's dead already. Spared feeling his body burn. The excruciating pain. Choking on the stench of his own charred flesh. Spared surviving, & whatever that would have meant: waking up in a hospital in traction, head & body bandaged, maybe an eyehole, maybe not, unable to remember anything that happened, unable to recognize Susan & Angela, or remember they ever existed, perhaps trying to pretend he knows them.

There are worse things than having a husband die.

All the same, after the dream Susan always stays awake & plays solitaire for the rest of the night.

SUSAN

Angela says she doesn't think it's a bat.

Susan cringes. She has never considered bats. She should have. In the park each evening, dark shadows swoop from tree to tree. Susan ties a scarf around her hair. Even so, as they dart past, she ducks & lets out a little scream, then feels foolish.

Susan is teaching T.S. Eliot at school. In 'The Waste Land':

> *...bats with baby faces in the violet light*
> *whistled...*

She has never heard bats whistle. It's just as well. She is terrified enough already.

Susan hopes the noises are made by something else. Anything. Mice, maybe.

But Angela doesn't think they're mice either. *Sometimes the sounds are gentle,* she says, *more like a bird. Maybe one is stuck behind a joist & will have to stay there until it dies.* Susan thinks about Angela having to listen to its last sounds.

Even so, Susan wouldn't mind so much having birds. They are innocuous enough for her to consider without flinching, even though they make a mess, even though neighbours all around her put out fake owls to scare off pigeons. If something has to be in the attic, better birds than anything else.

Did you ever see that Hitchcock movie? Angela asks, & they are quiet as they remember.

Writing fiction is so much easier than coping with real life.

Cassie likes working in Civilizations. It's easier than helping her mother around the house.

She gets paid. It seems so silly. She would pay them to let her be here.

She learns to make small talk with customers as she dishes out their food. She finds it easy now to start a conversation.

Cassie can handle anything: choir practice Tuesday nights, working at Civilizations after school, visiting her grandparents on weekends.

Her grades don't suffer, even though she arrives tired at school each day because animals above her bedroom ceiling disturb her sleep. *Do something,* she tells her mother who teaches school all day & reads books every night, & in between, stares out windows.

SUSAN

Susan's memory is inconvenient. A projector plays the same scene over & over inside her mind. It happened several months ago:

She goes to the doctor for something minor, a flu bug that refuses to go away.

I've been under a lot of stress, Susan tells him. *I'm probably run down.*

Everyone has this flu. Get lots of rest. It'll go away.

She gets ready to leave. *I used to dream about the accident every night,* she says, *but not any more. That valium you gave me helped.*

Good.

It was such a shock though. Having him die so suddenly. Anyway, I think I'm finally getting used to it. It's been a year now.

Maybe it wasn't such a bad way to die. The doctor's voice sounds reassuring. *Cancer's a lot worse.*

Cancer?

Oh, he says. *You didn't know.*

Cancer. Her husband had it. He knew, & didn't tell her.

CASSIE

Stop trying to get my father & me together, Cassie tells her grandmother. *I never want to see him again.*

Cassie doesn't mention that her father comes to Civilizations every weekend & tries to make small talk, how he watches her whenever he thinks she's not looking. Maybe if she doesn't tell anyone that he comes to the restaurant, he will stop.

It wasn't your fault, you know, her grandmother tells her.

Maybe it was. How do I know?

No, her grandmother insists. *Don't blame yourself. It was never about you at all. It wasn't your fault your daddy left. It wasn't your fault about your momma's drinking & the way she kept taking tranquillizer pills.*

Then whose fault was it? Cassie asks.

Oh lordy, I don't know, her grandmother says. *Possibly it was mine. I watched, but couldn't keep it from happening.*

Stop it, says Cassie, grabbing her tight. *Please just stop it, stop it, stop it. Don't pretend it was your fault. It wasn't your marriage. What could you do?*

It wasn't your marriage either, says her grandmother.

I'm sick of worrying about my parents. It happened so long ago. I wish I could just forget it.

They hug a minute & then Cassie notices the time. *Oh no. I've got to run. I'll be late for work.*

DAVID

David watches his father die. It seems to be taking forever.

He watches, & thinks, this seems to be some kind of family tradition. In a family that avoids traditions, this is one they haven't been able to discard, although they've tried. Fathers disappear. One day you see them, the next you don't. They walk out a door, turn a corner & are gone. They turn up once in a while & then disappear again. Years go by. Then they finally come home to die. They always return for this occasion, the way members of other families show up at birthdays or Christmas or Thanksgiving.

He watches his father die. His father watched his own father, & so on.

David thinks about his daughter. Some day Cassie will watch him die, or she won't. It all depends.

SUSAN

Cancer. The big C.

Susan buys daffodils each spring to support whatever the cancer society does. Research probably. Providing information. Giving support.

Susan could use some support herself.

Once she'd had a cancer scare that turned out to be nothing. She leaned on her husband's shoulder at the time. Of course she did. Who else would she turn to?

He was there when she needed him; she'd have liked to be there for him.

He didn't even tell her. She wants to confront him about it, grab him & shake him, holler, *Why not?*

He must have needed comfort. Did he get it somewhere else? Not from Susan anyway. He didn't need her.

Susan forces herself to think of noises above Angela's ceiling. They are easier to cope with.

She would switch beds with Angela & listen, but there's no point. They both know nothing would wake Susan up. She sleeps soundly to keep from thinking. She uses valium to do this.

SUSAN

It's 9:45 on Saturday morning. Susan sits at a corner table in Civilizations where she can watch whatever happens.

People eat breakfast: chocolate croissants or danish pastries, scrambled eggs on whole-wheat toast. They read their morning papers. They drink coffee. Second cups are half-price; all the customers have them.

Susan watches the line-up at the take-out. Local shopkeepers grab muffins & coffees to keep going through the morning. They chat back & forth about the weather, knowing how much it matters.

Wasn't last weekend the pits? All that rain.

Yeah. Why couldn't it have waited until Monday? Nothing happens on Mondays anyway.

Today's got to be better. I didn't make enough last Saturday to pay my staff.

How's the new clerk working out?

Not bad. But she's bright & won't last long. She'll move on.

Yeah. Better enjoy it while you can. Maybe get away a couple of days, like the rest of the world.

Can't afford it.

Yeah. Tell me about it. Who can?

Small shops straggle along the street. Hopeful people open them up, & a year later close them down. Brown paper covers the front window. In huge red letters, GOING OUT OF

BUSINESS or FINAL SALE. Then new signs replace them, OPENING SOON, UNDER NEW MANAGEMENT, & the whole cycle begins again. Susan hates shopping in these places. She begins to care about the owners, begins to think she ought to buy things inside their stores, whether she wants to or not. She feels guilty whenever she shops at the chain stores in the mall. She doesn't want to hear the store-owner conversations as they buy their take-out coffees. She doesn't want to know they can't afford to get away.

But this is research. She has to do it.

She can write them into her story, give it a feel of gritty reality. She needs to understand this neighbourhood to make her setting seem authentic.

Cassie stands behind the counter & listens to them talk. Did her father worry like this about his business when he was alive? Did he complain about it to her mother? Is this the way they talked together? She wishes she could re-member.

Her mother used to talk about him, but now she won't. Cassie wants to know their stories. What if her mother dies suddenly? It could happen. Her father ate breakfast with them one morning before a sales trip; a couple of days later he was dead. If her mother dies too, all their stories will be lost. Their ancestors. Cassie's history.

People search through old graveyards for ancestors they can't remember. Cassie has started to do this. Each time she visits her father's grave he seems farther & farther away. She's afraid to visit it any more for fear his memory will disappear completely.

She thinks it's because the coffin was kept closed. Her mother refused to open it up even though Cassie begged & begged to see him.

Remember him the way he was, her mother told her. *You wouldn't know him because of the burns.*

Her mother talked to her as though she was a child. As though she didn't know the gas tank exploded. He was thrown out of the car though. Probably he wasn't burned that much. She would have recognized him. He was her father & she'd have known him.

Maybe we're burying somebody else, she told her mother, *a hitchhiker he picked up.*

I saw him, her mother said. *It's your father. Remember him the way he was when he was alive.*

Some days Cassie can't remember what he looked like. She rushes home to check the photo on her dresser. Her father is black & white & shiny, just the same as always.

DAVID

David checks the supper tray. Ground beef. Mashed potatoes. Grey peas. Grey gravy. Vanilla pudding. A pot of water. No tea-bag.

Dammit, he thinks. He mutters it over & over, *Dammit, dammit, dammit,* all the way down the hall to the nursing station, where he is pleasant, where he smiles politely as he reports this absence of tea-bag, as though this is the first time, as though this doesn't happen at least once a week.

He suspects it's an economy measure. Trays at random get tea-bags, other trays don't. Old people propped up in bed, unable to mutter, *Dammit dammit dammit,* all the way to the nursing station. Needing sons & daughters to complain for them. Not having them on hand. Drinking hot water instead.

The thought of drinking hot water makes David feel sick.

Once he was a child & had a grandmother who drank hot water & chewed senna leaves every morning. *It keeps you open,* she told him. At the time he had no idea what she meant. *Never drink cold water in the morning,* she said.

Why did she take the hot water & senna leaves separately? he wonders now. Why didn't she make senna tea? Whenever he stayed there overnight he chewed a dry leaf too, & tried to drink hot water. This old memory of senna leaves. Where does it come from? he wonders. How does it turn up in some pants-pocket in his mind, to be jingled a bit, taken out, examined, & then put back.

Like old photographs in his bureau drawer, yellow, curling around the edges, snapshots he'd like to throw away. He looks at the people in the pictures & doesn't recognize them at all. Even though names are scribbled on the back in pencil: *Gran*, *Davey*.

Anyway, some day Cassie might want the snapshots.

David grabs a tea-bag at the nursing station & goes back to feed his father.

SUSAN

Susan moved into this old house a couple of months ago &
hoped it might be easy, but it's not. Feeling it out, learning its
rhythms. She wanted to leave her husband's ghost behind her,
but is surrounded by strangers' ghosts instead. Footsteps pace
to & fro, creak up & down the stairs. She hears someone
breathing heavily in the hall beyond her bedroom door. A toilet
runs awhile, then suddenly stops. The furnace turns off & on
according to some pattern of its own. A tap drips, a regular
heartbeat rhythm.

There are logical reasons for these noises to happen. Susan
is a teacher & knows this. She wonders whether the sounds
Angela hears might be structural. Perhaps nails gradually un-
fasten, groaning slightly as this happens. Nails that are tired of
supporting the dangling walls, walls that were designed to have
something to rest on. Floors should extend beneath the walls
to support them. A hundred years ago a builder economized
on hardwood. But it doesn't matter. The nails would finally
rust out anyway, Susan thinks. Plaster will give away, walls
collapse in a heap around her, & bats from the attic sweep
round & round her head.

If she really believes this will happen, she should move
outside, sleep on the porch, & make Angela sleep there too.
When she enters the house on an errand, she should tie a scarf
around her head.

Except bats live outside too.

Bats hang upside-down from the branches of trees. Susan imagines bats lined up in the attic, dangling from the rafters, like black mittens on a clothesline.

CASSIE

So many people work in Civilizations. Cassie's slowly getting to know them. Sometimes they tell her about their lives. Cassie is surprised when adults do this. She looks older than 18; that must be why. They have problems; their lives are like the soaps. Cassie's astonished; she always thought other families were perfect. These people tell stories that amaze her.

Their jobs here are only jobs. Their lives outside are what's important. Their families matter: a mother falls & breaks her hip, a husband drinks too much, a wife is pregnant, a kid gets expelled from school.

One woman asks, *Can you lend me 10 bucks till the weekend? My husband drank up my pay cheque again.*

Another wears dark glasses & has a boyfriend who beats her up. Everyone worries about her. Why does she stay with him? they wonder. No one can understand it. Should they report it to the police? Some say yes & some say no. They can't decide.

Only the adults discuss problems. The teenagers act like they haven't a worry in the world. Sometimes they complain about their homework, but half-heartedly, as though they only grumble because everyone expects it. They seem happy.

For instance Michael. He just seems normal.

Cassie wonders whether people look at her & see someone normal too.

SUSAN

Susan spends her professional development day in Civilizations watching people come in the door. She watches strangers who stop to read the menu. She watches the regulars who head straight for the counter & ask for soup-of-the-day & a garden salad with house dressing, or fettucini & a caesar salad with lots of parmesan cheese & olives, or strawberries & cottage cheese with an oatmeal muffin, or perhaps they pass by all the shiny foods & pour a cup of coffee, regular or decaf. They know exactly what they're doing.

Susan watches them; she feels part of it all, but also separate, an observer. This is the way she thinks all writers must feel, watching things around them, sometimes writing them down.

Cassie isn't here.

There is a man Susan sometimes watches. He doesn't show up.

Cassie grabs the tongs & serves caesar salad onto a plate. She remembers when her mother used to make it. Her father was alive then. He barbecued steaks in the backyard. Her mother made caesar salad with homemade croutons & homemade dressing. Homemade! Cassie tries to remember the last time her mother cooked anything. Now she heats up frozen TV dinners, brings home fried chicken, phones for pizza. A year ago Cassie's father died. It's been a year since homemade anything. Cassie is old enough to cook. It's just as well.

A different cashier is on duty. Where is the real Cassie? Susan wonders.

SUSAN

Forget the birds, Mom, says Angela. *If any birds are up there, they're in addition to something else.* The noises are getting louder, & wake Angela every morning at 5 a.m.

Remember when we still had Skippy? Angela asks. *How I'd throw a tennis ball, & he'd bound around the living room trying to catch it, tripping, crashing into the furniture & walls?*

It drove me crazy.

Yeah. You'd yell at us to be quiet. Anyway, that's what it sounds like above my head. Something runs up one side of the window & down the other. It's something big. It must be as big as a middle-sized dog.

You always exaggerate. Nothing small enough to fit between the walls could possibly make that much noise. Hyperbole. Teenagers always exaggerate for effect. Susan certainly hopes so.

Anyway, it's not a bird, says Angela. *Trust me, Mom. It's something big. Maybe we've got raccoons like the neighbours.*

Raccoons live in the house next door. Susan & Angela can sit outside in the evening & watch them emerge in single file, then amble across fences, porches, gardens. They live inside a basement entrance, up high, behind a beam. The guy who rents the basement apartment finds them unnerving. As he walks down his stairs he always sees them. When he reaches the third step down, they are right ahead of him at eye level, their paws lined up along the edge of the wood, their bright eyes watching. He laughs about it to Susan & Angela, but he's looking for another flat.

Susan can't imagine trying to get rid of raccoons. They're not afraid of anything. If she yells at the ones next door, they stare at her as though she's acting stupid, & then carry on with whatever they are doing.

On the other hand, the woman next door says one of the raccoons ambled inside the house through an open doorway, & their cat hissed at it & snarled & was able to chase it out.

Susan reads about them: *raccoon* can be spelled with two c's or one. *Did you know that?* she asks the guy next door. He doesn't care.

Susan picks up an old newspaper at a garage sale & discovers an article about raccoons:

> *...they were in Toronto before the Indians. Two or three million years before, in fact... they drifted south with other wild beasts when the glaciers arrived and the only sound in Toronto was the wind whistling over mile-thick ice...*

I think I've got raccoons, she tells one of the teachers at school, & he tells her a raccoon story. He keeps his dog in the backyard while he's at work. The dog's a nice big gentle mutt that never gets in fights. It's so big the other dogs leave it alone. One day a raccoon climbed inside the fence & terrorized the dog. The man came home & found it whimpering. The dog wasn't injured but its spirit was broken. *My dog's never been the same since,* he tells Susan. *It gets frantic every morning when I get ready to leave for work.* He shakes his head sadly as he remembers.

I thought raccoons were nocturnal, Susan says.

Once in a while you see them in the daytime. Not often though. So we were afraid this one might be rabid. Luckily it wasn't.

Susan tries to imagine something in her attic that could terrorize a big dog. It's not so hard. After all, she herself is terrified at the possibility of bats or tiny mice.

Not everyone minds raccoons. One of Susan's neighbours loves them. She raises motherless kits in cages inside her house until they are large enough to manage outside on their own. Susan wonders whether the woman is really doing the raccoons a favour. Will they always try to move back inside? Is she doing her neighbours a favour? After all, they will have to provide the free accommodation.

There are things Cassie's mother will tell her, as soon as she figures out what they are. Or maybe not. Maybe she won't need to invent plausible stories.

Look at Cassie. She is strong & beautiful & perfect. She doesn't need fairy tales to survive on. She smiles at customers as though they matter. She prepares their sandwiches exactly the way they want them

Feeding. Nurturing. This seems to be what women's lives are all about.

Will she tell Cassie about her father's cancer? Maybe. Maybe not.

Will I ever tell Angela? Susan wonders. Maybe. When she's old enough, whenever that is.

DAVID & CASSIE

David walks into Civilizations for Sunday brunch. Cassie is usually working. Sometimes she'll speak to him, sometimes she won't. She either smiles at him or frowns. When she smiles he tries not to show he's pleased, because it probably means nothing; she smiles at all the other customers too.

David pretends to read the newspaper while he watches his daughter ignore him. She might come over on her break & ask how her grandfather is, or she might not. *Come with me sometime,* David suggests. She always refuses. But sometimes Cassie drops in to see her grandfather right after school when she knows David is still at work. David doesn't tell her he knows about the visits; it seems to be a secret. His father can't tell him, & Cassie won't. The nurses always mention it though. They tell David she is beautiful. She looks just like her mother, is what he thinks.

After David left them, Cassie & her mother moved in with her grandmother. Cassie was 12 years old. He wonders what they told her, & has never been able to find out. Eventually her mother moved in with someone else, but Cassie stayed on at her grandmother's. *You don't need me,* she told David. *Grandma does. Anyway, you were the one that moved away in the first place. You were the one who wanted out.*

David remembers being a child, & the relief whenever his father left. Some nights he'd wake up in a panic for fear his father had come back. He'd listen to the silence, not trusting it, then check that his mother was okay before he tried to get back to sleep. He'd asked them both later why they'd stayed together so long. He thought they'd probably stuck it out for his sake. His martyr-mother, it's the sort of thing she would do. But David waited too long to ask his father who had forgotten almost everything. His mother hardly understood the question. *You get married, you stay married*, she told him. Like an old expression David remembered from long ago, *You make your bed & then lie in it.* It was that, & it was also who his mother was. Not a quitter. Someone who believed in families, that everyone belonged inside one, like a fortress.

Did you still love him? David had persisted. *Is that why you stayed with him?* But apparently love had nothing to do with it. She seemed to think the question was irrelevant.

She looked at him as though he was crazy. *Where would I have taken you?* she asked. *How would we eat?* The practicalities.

Once, when he was very young, he thought his parents should live together. Of course. They should do it for his sake. He needed both of them & they should be there. How young must he have been? Terribly young.

He still thinks this about parents, but in the abstract. Not his own mother & father. Not himself & his ex-wife.

It was different for your mom & me, he tells Cassie.

How was it different? she asks him.

He doesn't know.

Other parents manage to stay together, she says. *They make a promise when they get married, & don't change their minds later on.*

Maybe they do it for their kids' sake. Kids need them & they should be there.

I had to go. It would have been worse if I'd been there. I couldn't stay & watch her.

SUSAN

Susan wonders what the name Cassie stands for. Probably Cassandra.

No one calls her Cassandra, of course, except her mother. Mothers always call children by their correct names. *How could you give me such a stupid name?* Cassie always asks her mother. Even though she knows the answer. Even though she knows she was named after her Aunt Cassie who died in childbirth. Both Aunt Cassie & her baby died. Cassie thinks about that little baby never having a chance at all. Sometimes she feels as though she's a replacement for the baby, & hates being stuck with the baby's mother's name, a name no one in their right mind would ever want, a name she tells no one, but people sometimes figure it out. *Cassie?* they ask. *What does it mean? Is it short for something?* They think of other words, casserole, castanets, Casablanca, & finally come up with Cassandra. Sometimes they tell her about the other Cassandra, the one in books. Cassie has heard it all a thousand times before & wants to scream, but she doesn't. Not yet.

This is what fiction is, Susan thinks. Taking a real name & making up the rest of the details. She thinks of Angela, Angelina really, named after her dead aunt. Angela hates her name too.

Cassie goes home & yells at her mother about how it's a stupid crazy name, & as soon as she's old enough she's going to change it. She hasn't decided on a new name yet. It must be perfect. She has criteria. She can't know anyone else who has it. It can't belong to a famous person or someone in a book or on TV. It can't be shortened to something crude. It must go with almost any last name, including the one she already has, the last name she wants to change, as soon as she can find the perfect boyfriend. She hasn't found him yet. She works part-time in Civilizations. Maybe she'll find him there.

Maybe Susan will meet somebody there too. She thinks of this as she tries to concentrate on her writing. If it is possible for the character in the story, if it will be believable, then why not? She knows why not. The girl she writes about is 16. Susan is 44; 30 years is 30 years is 30 years.

There is this man though; sometimes she sees him in Civilizations, but of course she only watches him in order to write him into her story.

SUSAN

Susan has broken her valium tablets in half; she wakes up now in the middle of the night, wakens & notices she is listening. She tiptoes along the hall to Angela's door. The floor creaks beneath her bare feet. The wind rattles branches against the house. Ordinary sounds drift in Angela's window. Music. Rustling leaves. Cars. Voices.

Susan realizes she has a love-hate relationship with nature. Animals & birds are easier to like inside a zoo, beyond a window. Up close they intimidate her. She is taller & outweighs them, but it doesn't matter; she's outnumbered & afraid.

She wants to live inside boundaries that exclude them. The walls & roof of her house should do it, but are apparently inadequate. In *Never Cry Wolf* the hero urinated all around a campsite. Susan would collect a bottle of pee & drizzle it along the outside of her house if she thought it would help.

She wants to bang her daughter's ceiling & drive the creatures up there crazy. She wants to holler at them, *Get out. This is my house. I have to pay the mortgage & taxes. Angela & I need peace & quiet. We deserve it.*

But it is the middle of the night. She makes a pot of tea instead & sits in the kitchen with her notebook.

Cassie looks at her mother & wonders who she is. A teacher. A mother. A widow. Nothing else.

In the evenings she marks papers or reads books.

Do something, Cassie tells her. *Go somewhere. See people.*

Her mother says she's too tired.

Susan can't holler at the animals because Angela is asleep. Finally she goes to bed. There is nothing in the attic. She tries to believe this.

SUSAN

The noises keep on happening, & Angela gets more & more upset. *Do something*, she tells her mother. *If it chews its way into my bedroom I'll leave home.* Susan doesn't blame her. She won't stay inside the house herself.

The man across the street talks to everyone. Susan can't avoid him; he's always out front when she comes home from work. Painting his porch, sweeping his sidewalk, digging weeds out of the lawn. Susan mentions the animal noises to him & he tells her about the time he met a skunk.

Coming home late at night he saw an animal ripping open a garbage bag. He thought of all the times he'd picked up garbage from bags that dogs had ripped open, from garbage cans they'd tipped over. Now, he had caught one in the act. He kicked at it as he went past, even though he loves dogs & owns one, even though he's basically a non-violent person. Just as his foot struck the animal he noticed the white stripe. Then: gasping, suffocating, his skin & eyes on fire. The pain. Being blind. Afraid he might never see again. The terrible burning in his throat, & revolting taste that made him retch. Being unable to eat for days, unable to get out of bed for a week.

Would a skunk climb three flights up? Susan asks him. He doesn't know. She reads about them just in case.

Skunk comes from American Indian. Susan finds two spellings, segankw & segongw. They both seem unpronounceable;

no wonder the colonists selected skunk. The word is also used as a verb, meaning to beat badly, to really trounce. She knew this but had forgotten. In some game she played long ago with her husband there was a skunk line. Cribbage, maybe.

People are as welcome as a skunk at a garden party when they aren't welcome at all. Susan can remember an aunt using that old expression, can't imagine the aunt at a garden party though. It seems too British, too snobby & upper class: reception lines, white gloves, waiters, silver platters, sandwiches with crusts off (perhaps cook will make bread pudding tomorrow), open-face sandwiches cut into fancy shapes, spread with cream cheese, a layer of cucumber or watercress, olive slices or caviar positioned carefully on top. Then the arrival of a skunk.

She remembers Flower the skunk, Bambi's friend. Children loved him.

Susan daydreams of writing a book as popular as *Bambi*.

CASSIE & DAVID

Each time Cassie sees her father in Civilizations she hates him a little less or she likes him a little more. He is trying. She's afraid he might be winning.

She understands the way his mind works: if she gets used to seeing me around maybe she'll forgive me, & the missing years won't matter.

He tells Cassie he always wanted to see her, but the idea made her mother get even more upset. He was afraid of what would happen if she had a breakdown. Her grandmother tells her the same thing. Cassie doesn't believe them.

The years are gone now, & they mattered. That's what no one seems to understand.

The restaurant is crowded. A woman in the line-up sends a little girl to hold a table. The child fidgets there awhile, & finally goes & stands behind her mother.

Of course the table is taken by someone else.

Dana! Now there's nowhere to sit! When I tell you to do something you've got to do it. What am I supposed to do with all this food while we wait for another table? The tray's heavy. This is all your fault! Next time do what you're told!

Cassie keeps watching them & looks like she might cry.

David watches Cassie watch the mother & child. We did better than that, David thinks. He hopes Cassie knows it.

Probably not.

CASSIE & SUSAN

There is a woman Cassie sees in Civilizations, an English teacher from school. On weekends she sits in a corner with a notebook & writes things down. She looks like she knows what she is doing. She wouldn't have time to sit & write if she had problems in her life. Cassie wishes her mother would do this, sit here & drink coffee & write down bits of information. Cassie would read each piece of paper & be able to understand her.

What are you writing? Cassie finally asks the woman.

A novel.

Cassie can't imagine how the woman does it. She seems to have all the time in the world. She can concentrate while confusion is all around her. Songs on the radio. Babies crying. Conversations. She seems to enjoy the noise.

Cassie says, *I thought all the people who wrote books were already dead*, & then regrets it.

The woman laughs. Luckily she has a sense of humour.

Susan sits down at a table & starts to write. She has to. She has told this young girl she's writing a novel. Now she has to really do it. She has never confessed her dream to anyone before.

Cassie stands behind the counter. She wears her hair pulled into a pony tail even though it makes her look like she's a child. But the uniform makes a difference. She wears a blue & white striped smock, & looks like she knows what she is doing. The customers seem to believe this; Cassie almost believes it herself.

At first someone helps her, shows her how to make a strawberry milkshake, an egg salad sandwich on whole wheat. It is easy, & seems as unreal, as unrelated to the ordinary meals she used to eat at home, as her cooking assignments in family studies class at school.

Now, though, her mother never cooks anything; she picks up cold meat on the way home from work, or phones for pizza. *What's for dinner?* Cassie asks, & her mother looks puzzled. *Dinner?*

Cassie hates to cook at home. She shouldn't have to. What are mothers for anyway? Her mother is supposed to enjoy it. Cassie can't imagine wanting to cook for a husband & children. They couldn't be worth it. Preparing meals 365 days a year, year after year. Her mother seemed to enjoy it at the time. She must have been crazy. She never wanted any help. Cassie would have helped out in the kitchen if her mother had ever asked.

Cassie remembers when her father was alive & her mother found it possible to cook. Cassie was able to take meals for granted.

Susan closes her notebook. She's tired of writing. She feels like going home & baking something special, but there's no point. Angela isn't home.

SUSAN

Susan haunts the library. She reads of animals under porches, in attics, behind walls. She reads of poisons & traps. Of animals with rabies, scabies, ticks, fleas, lice, internal parasites. Of ants, wasps, cockroaches, silverfish, termites. She reads & is afraid to go home.

Susan switches to the literature section instead. She looks up household pests in poetry anthologies. Poets commemorate them. *The Pied Piper of Hamelin.* Susan could use a pied piper herself.

In children's stories, animals have anthropomorphic attributes. Susan re-reads Grey Owl, Ernest Thompson Seton, Mother Goose. The Thornton Burgess books: *Jimmy Skunk, Chatterer the Red Squirrel, Bobby Coon.*

She reads Don Marquis: Archy the cockroach & Mehitabel the alley cat are reincarnations of people. Susan wonders what's in her attic & who it used to be.

She reads a poem by Don Coles about how groundhogs view people. She wishes he would write from the perspective of an animal inside an attic. Someone should suggest it, assure him there'd be an urban market.

CASSIE

A customer pays for a pineapple milkshake. Suddenly Cassie slips inside some memory from her childhood: her father making an ice-cream soda. Hot days in the summer. A wading pool in the backyard. Cassie & her mother & father sitting on plastic lawn chairs, soaking their feet in the wading pool, sipping cool drinks from frosted glasses. Cassie wonders where those glasses went.

Were her parents happy then, or did she just assume they were? She was only a small child. What would she notice? What would she care anyway? They were her parents. They were supposed to stay with her & be her family.

Her father. He never says anything he means. Anyway they have nothing to talk about.

He used to come to the house to visit. Cassie always ignored him, & her grandmother talked to him instead. Finally he stopped coming, but he drops by the restaurant every weekend while she's at work. He reads a book or a newspaper & only speaks to her when he pays for his coffee.

Why does he keep coming? She hardly speaks to him but he shows up again anyway. Does he expect some miracle to happen & make it easy for them to communicate?

The awkwardness is her fault; she doesn't trust him. Of course not. He walked out once; he could easily betray her trust again.

Cassie used to think the divorce was her fault too. Partly she still believes this. It wouldn't have happened if she'd been good enough, if she'd kept quiet, cleaned her room... Whatever it was, she should have done it. Sometimes she wonders which thing was the final straw, what sin she could have committed important enough to break them up. There's no point asking. They'd just deny it.

All kids think divorce is their fault. Cassie knows this; she reads books & watches TV. Cassie wants to shake those kids & tell them they're crazy; of course it's not their fault; it's their stupid parents. All the same she still feels that way herself.

Sometimes she wonders if she was wanted, if she was planned. There's no use asking her mother, who gets uncomfortable when questions get intimate. Years ago Cassie asked her to describe what having sex felt like, but her mother pretended not to hear.

Her grandmother talks in platitudes: *Save yourself for your husband. Why should he buy the cow if he can get the milk for nothing? You make your bed & then lie in it.*

DAVID

David is using his pleasant tone of voice, the one he reserves for his dying father, & for a small child when he had one. The child grew up into a young woman who seems to hate him. Perhaps Cassie would like him if he used a different tone of voice. There may be words she waits for him to say; he has no idea what they are.

Mashed potatoes, Dad. Open your mouth. That's right. Vanilla pudding. Open your mouth. Okay now. A sip of tea.

A slurp of tea. Tea dribbles down his father's chin, onto his shirt. No matter how careful David is, this always happens. Another slurp of tea, a few more drips. His father smacking his lips. His father almost saying something. *Good,* is what David imagines his father would say, if his father was able to talk. Or maybe, *Thanks. Thanks for being such a good son.*

He hands his father the piece of white bread, looks away, can't bear to watch him hide it beneath the pillow. All over the building old people do this. Nurses find bread crusts in the morning when they make the beds. Perhaps they scold. But why would they bother? After all, what does it matter.

SUSAN

Susan sips a cup of coffee & watches the restaurant door. There is a man who comes into Civilizations once in a while. She would like to write him into her story. It would seem like writing him into her life.

A gang of retired cronies takes up one end of the restaurant. They shout back & forth from one table to another. Apparently all of them are deaf. Or a few are, so they got into the habit of shouting. Probably their deafness happened right here in Civilizations, & was caused by all their voices hollering against each other's ear drums.

They yak constantly but say nothing. They talk to make contact & to exercise their mouths:

Hey Charlie. Seen Evelyn lately? I think maybe she's gone away.

A smoker's hacking cough, & then an answer, *Nope. Not for a while. But Ronnie's gone off to visit his daughter. We'll see how long that lasts.*

Which one? That rich one, or the other?

I forgot there was so many. The one he always fights with.

Good old Ronnie. You can't let them start pushing you around. They start shoving & never stop.

Like Wilbur.

Wilbur? Which one's he?

You know. The squirrel guy. The one that sits in the park & feeds squirrels. Or is it pigeons?

Susan listens closely. She would like to be able to write conversations this authentic. She would like to be able to talk that way herself.

Isn't he William?

Hey Rosie. Remember the guy with the green plaid jacket that feeds squirrels or pigeons or something? Is he Wilbur or is he William? Do you remember?

For God's sake, Mabel, don't ask me. I put the dog out in the morning, & can't remember his name to call him back.

Yeah, I can hardly remember the names of my kids. Of course it'd help if I ever saw them.

That's kids for you.

Yeah. Feed them & grow them up & then forget them. It's the only way.

The way the world works.

Yep. The fast pace. No one has any time. Just work, work, work. Or play, play, play.

Not like the old days, eh Rosie? Imagine our mothers ever letting us get away with that.

Not my mother. No way. She never put up with anything. Even when I was grown up & away from home & married, if I didn't call her twice a day she'd go on & on about it. She'd keep complaining until I did.

They holler from one table to another. Their voices surround Susan. She can't decide whether to include this kind of background chatter in her novel. It wouldn't move the story along, but would add some colour. Susan tries to ignore them;

she assumes that all around the restaurant other customers are trying to do this too. It is something they have in common.

Susan feels sorry for the staff. They must get sick & tired of hearing the same conversations over & over. These old people are so boring. Susan can't imagine how they were able to get so old without learning anything interesting to mention. Unless they've already told each other everything of interest inside their minds, & nothing's left. Like conversations in an old marriage.

What must Cassie think about them? Susan wonders. How does she talk to them at the cash desk? Does she let her feelings show?

And the boy who clears the tables. What must he think? Michael. The boy Cassie always glances at, always pretends not to notice. What about him? He can't avoid them. He has to go back & forth past them all the time. They try to draw him into their conversation. *What about you Michael?* they ask, putting him on the spot. *What do you think about this? Am I right or is he?*

Susan watches them, & wonders if this is where she's going, if this is how she'll be in another 20 or 30 years.

A young couple across from Susan manages to ignore them. Susan has seen them here before. She remembers the first time she saw them, how sweet she thought they were, how terribly shy. They looked everywhere but at each other, but when the boy went for more coffee the girl watched him; when the girl went to get an extra serviette the boy's eyes followed her. That initial shyness is over. Now they touch each other all the time, their hands wander, their legs twine beneath the table. Susan wishes for god's sake they'd go home. Presumably each one has a home to go to, or they have one together. Surely they can find some place more private where Susan doesn't have to watch.

She remembers that stage. Not being able to take your eyes away, or your hands. The pain of not touching. Memories she'd rather forget.

Cassie tells her mother to go out for heaven's sake. Do something. Meet someone, meaning a man.

Perhaps she does this for her mother's sake. Or for her own, so she can go out with men when she is ready, her mother not glancing up sadly from her book, her mother happily distracted with her own plans.

We do the right things, Susan thinks, for the wrong reasons.

SUSAN

Meanwhile there is still something in the attic. Someone knows what to do about it. Susan discusses the noises with everyone in order to find that person. Everyone she meets has animal stories; they tell them & tell them until Susan feels even worse.

They tell her to call a trapper. She doesn't want to.

Finally, though, Susan phones one. Even though it seems an acknowledgment of defeat. Angela is right: something lives inside this house that Susan had wanted to feel safe in.

She phones in a rare decisive moment, knowing something must be done, & there's no one else to do it. A taped message answers & rambles on & on. Susan hangs up.

The next time Angela complains Susan can always say she called a trapper, but didn't like the message on his answering machine. *One of those chatty ones*, she'll tell Angela. *You know how much I hate them.*

She imagines Angela's reaction, & phones back.

The trapper returns her call that evening. Susan expects him to figure out over the phone what kind of animal or bird or bat she's got, but he can't, which makes her wonder, how good is this guy anyway?

When the trapper looks at the side of the house, he says, *Well lady, you've got squirrels all right. No doubt about it.*

Squirrels, Susan thinks. Of course. She should have

thought of them herself. After all, there are oak trees everywhere. That's the first thing she liked about this place.

The trapper points out the place where they get in. *That's the kind of hole a squirrel makes*, he tells her. Finally Susan sees it, in the soffit, just below the top peak of the roof, at the side of the house, three storeys straight up.

Not enough space to put up a ladder between these houses, the trapper's saying.

Susan looks & realizes there isn't. Her house is tall & skinny, & set so close to the one next door there's barely room to walk between them. The opening looks impossible to get to, even for squirrels, & certainly for humans who rely on ladders.

The trapper checks the upstairs windows, but the hole is still inaccessible. *Smart little buggers*, he says, in admiration.

Susan wonders what this means. Will she have to learn to love her squirrels? Feed Angela valium each night?

The trapper makes up his mind. A ladder from her neighbour's backyard will reach the roof of a second-floor sunroom; from there he can climb up the third-floor roof & put a trap right at the peak. He'll place it where Susan can see it from the ground. She's to phone whenever the trap is sprung & he'll replace it with another.

Susan imagines him shinnying up to the peak of the roof. He's bound to fall. She doesn't want to watch, or even know when it is happening. She can't handle the responsibility. She hates his taped message, but that's not enough reason to kill him.

Forget it, she says. *It's too dangerous.*

You can't leave them in your house, he tells her. *They'll eat your wiring. It's not safe.*

Susan imagines how long a piece of wiring would last if a squirrel decided to munch it. She's read about their teeth, the chisel-shaped incisors that keep growing like fingernails. Hard use keeps them worn down.

Anyway, the trapper continues, *imagine how filthy it will get. They'll be shitting inside there. It'll start to smell.*

Susan hires the trapper.

How many squirrels are in there? she asks.

Who knows? Three or four. Maybe less. Maybe more. I'll keep putting up empty traps until they stop getting sprung. When you stop hearing any noises, let me know & I'll seal up the hole.

What will happen to them?

Don't worry. The trap won't hurt them. I won't either. I'll put the traps in the back of the truck & drive north of the city before I let them out. There's a conservation area I go to. They won't find their way back.

In a wooded conservation area where there are no houses to move into, her squirrels will have to revert to ancestral habits of building nests in trees.

I'll bait the trap with peanut butter.

Squirrel? she asks.

He laughs. *Sure. Why not? It ought to be their favourite kind.*

Susan laughs with him. She can't wait to tell Angela what kind of peanut butter he's going to use. She can't wait to tell everyone.

Squirrels, she thinks. Good. If she has to have creatures in her attic, better squirrels than anything else. At least they're cute.

Susan has hired a trapper. She can hardly believe it. Angela will be happy & forgive her procrastination. Action has been taken.

DAVID & CASSIE

David pays Cassie for his coffee. *Hi, honey*, he says.

She hands him his change. *I don't understand how you could leave us*, she tells him.

A line-up of people is waiting. Is she deliberately trying to embarrass him? he wonders. Is that what she wants? Some kind of revenge?

David says, *Come over & talk to me on your break.*

Cassie says, *Maybe*, but doesn't bother.

SUSAN

Susan sits at Civilizations reading a newspaper that someone left behind. A headline mentions suicide.

Suddenly an awful thought crosses her mind: her husband, was that how he died?

Of course not. He always said he couldn't understand why people did it. They must be crazy.

Then again, why not? It would seem logical. Knowing he would die anyway, it would hardly seem like suicide at all.

She wants him back, to grab him & argue: *No. They might have cured it, excised it, you might have gone into remission. Anyway, having cancer doesn't change things. You, me, Angela, all of us are going to die anyway.*

He always loved to prove her wrong, would use the argument against her: *So? We're dying anyway? Then what's the difference? Suicide merely changes the day it happens.*

She's being foolish. He didn't run the car off the road deliberately. He wouldn't do that. If he'd felt depressed she'd have known it. He always told her what he was thinking, didn't have secrets.

It's not true though. He had cancer & never told her.

This man, the man she lived with, the father of her daughter: she wonders, did she ever know him at all?

Someone is asking, *Are you all right?* It's the girl named Cassie; she has her hand on Susan's shoulder.

IF I KNEW I'D TELL YOU

I'm fine, says Susan. It's hard to talk though, because she's crying.

She leaves quickly, walks to the park, finds a secluded bench. She watches squirrels gather acorns against the winter. Life goes on.

Anyway, what does it matter? Already she consults snapshots to remember what her husband looked like. If the creatures behind the walls chew the wiring & burn the house down, the photo album will be destroyed. Susan will be unable to remember him at all. She almost wishes it would happen.

CASSIE & DAVID

Why do you do it? Cassie asks. *Visit Grandpa every single night. Feed him. Take him for walks. Put him to bed. He has nurses there to help him.*

Or she tells David why he does it: To make himself feel good, ease his conscience. To make up for hurting her.

I happen to love him, says David.

You don't even know him. He walked out when you were a kid. You hardly ever saw him.

David knows she says this to make him feel bad. His father walked out when David was eight. David walked out when Cassie was 12. & so on, he thinks. Etcetera. Someday Cassie will understand, when she walks out on someone who loves her.

I always knew I could reach him if I had to, David says. Meaning: at least you've always had that.

If he'd been home when Cassie was younger he wouldn't have let her watch her favourite TV shows: re-runs of *Father Knows Best, Leave It To Beaver.* She wanted a perfect family, a bike, a paper route, a white frame house & picket fence, a rope swing hanging from an elm tree.

No, that's not true. HE wanted those things. HE wanted whatever the other kids had. These are the things he had to forgive his parents for not providing. He has no idea what

Cassie wanted. He knows what she says; it's not necessarily the same.

Perhaps she only wanted not to hate him.

CASSIE

Cassie watches Michael as he cleans tables. He's nice to everyone, even the old folks at tables in the corner, the loud ones that people either like or hate. He is polite to a woman who shoves a stroller in his way & almost trips him. He is pleasant to a little kid who runs back & forth & drives everyone crazy. Cassie waits for Michael to make some sarcastic remark about the kid when he goes past her at the cash desk, but he just winks & says the name of some castle. Last week he called her Casa Loma. Today it's Castle Frank. She wonders how many castle names he knows.

The other people who work here call her Cassie; but not Michael. She wonders why. If it was anyone else she'd think he was trying to attract her attention.

Anyway, he's already got it.

The teacher sits in a corner & keeps watching everything that happens. Sometimes she makes Cassie nervous. She watches Cassie, or sometimes Michael. Or she watches the doorway but pretends to be staring into space. Cassie wonders whether the woman waits for someone. She wishes the person would hurry up & get here so the woman will stop watching & write things down.

Cassie wants the teacher's novel to be finished. The book will be published & Cassie will find it in a bookstore. She will hold it in her hand & know she was there when it really happened.

SUSAN

Now Susan tells her friends she has squirrels & friends tell her their squirrel stories.

Gord had a squirrel in his attic. He stood on a ladder in the bedroom cupboard & slowly opened the trapdoor in the ceiling. Suddenly the squirrel jumped on his shoulder & ran into the bedroom, where Gord's wife was under the covers screaming. The squirrel was angry & upset. They all were. Gord chased it from room to room. It finally left through an open window...

Susan imagines a squirrel loose inside her house, Angela screaming, & Susan, being the mother, expected to know what to do about it.

She's glad to have turned the responsibility over to someone else. She wishes she'd asked the trapper for references, or checked with the Better Business Bureau, but it's too late now. She'll have to trust him.

CASSIE & DAVID

Why did you leave us? Cassie asks David. She asks this as though he planned his departure ahead of time, as though he ever plans anything. She asks him, as though she expects him to answer, to have the words to explain this, or anything.

You don't understand, he tells her. *I had to go.* He hides behind the tinted glasses that separate him from the world. *I can't tell you,* he says. *I want to, but I can't.* Or something like that.

Or you can, but you don't want to. Cassie fills in the missing blanks. It is worth it to see him almost smile.

He stares out the window. His left hand curled into a fist, his right hand rubs it until it relaxes. Cassie can feel his tension as he remembers how it was.

Maybe, he says.

Maybe what?

David looks startled. He looks as though he sees her from a million miles away. Puzzled, as though he met her once before & can almost remember who she is.

Why? she always asks him, not even knowing why she asks, whether it matters any more.

But she's afraid the same thing will happen again, that it runs in families: that she'll get married & have a child & do the same thing to her child that her father did to her. Meaning, nothing. Meaning, not being there. Meaning, leaving a helpless child behind.

How can she prevent it if she doesn't understand how it happens?

This is what she never tells anyone: There were times when she wanted to run away so her family couldn't find her. There are times when she still might.

SUSAN

The man Susan watches for has brown hair flecked with grey & a grey beard flecked with brown. They have seen each other often enough to nod or say hello. Whenever she enters Civilizations she checks the tables to see whether he's there. If he is, she pretends not to see him. If he isn't, she sits somewhere facing the door. When he enters he doesn't seem to see her. He gets his coffee, walks past her without a glance & places the cup on a table. Always he forgets he needs a creamer. He goes back & gets one, & as he returns to his table he suddenly glances at her & says hello. Lately she has begun to make some innocuous comment about the weather, *Nice day, eh?* or *Still raining out?* He never joins her at her table; Susan never suggests it. She is afraid to. It would be a giant step toward him, & hard to back off from. After all, she only wants to know him better in order to write him into her novel. Of course.

If she asked him to join her he would do it. He could hardly refuse. Next time he would take the invitation for granted. He would sit down at her table, obliging her to talk, to let her thoughts out into the air where he can hear them, to share something of who she is, as if she knows who she is these days, avoiding her house & the squirrels inside it, sitting in Civilizations, watching for this man, trying to write a novel, observing how life keeps happening around her, like seasons, like phases of the moon, like the way Angela keeps on growing up whether Susan wants her to or not.

What in the world would they talk about? Susan wonders. But they would talk. There are so many things they don't know about each other. They would keep talking & talking, not noticing the time. It wouldn't matter. She would have nothing else as important she should be doing; neither would he.

She doesn't want this to happen. They would touch. A neighbourly pat upon a shoulder, a friendly hand upon the arm. A touch she has been imagining, waiting for. They'd keep on touching & touching. There'd be no turning back.

Susan knows, if she ever starts to touch him she won't be able to stop.

She walks into Civilizations. The man is there. She ignores him.

DAVID & CASSIE

David buys a cup of coffee.

When did you make up your mind? Cassie asks him. *Was it after I left for school? Why didn't you even tell me? I came home from school & you were gone. It wasn't fair.*

He stares at her. What does she want from him anyway? The truth? A truth. Which one?

Why did you do it?

He doesn't care how many people are lined up behind him. He doesn't care who listens. *I had to go. Your mother made me furious. She stayed in her room all day long, drinking. Your grandma had to look after you. She came over every afternoon before you got home from school. Your mother would be still in the bedroom. Sleeping. Waking up & drinking some more. Dozing off again. Don't you remember what it was like? She refused to go to AA. Kept pretending she didn't have a problem. I'd come home & lose my temper.*

But that's not reason enough to leave us, says Cassie.

Okay then, thinks David. She wants to know this. Let's see if she can take it. *She made me so mad*, he confesses, *I was scared I'd hit her.*

There. He's never said the words before. He never intended to tell anyone. Especially not Cassie. His dark secret.

Probably it was the wrong thing to tell her. He doesn't want her to hate him any more than she does already. But anyway, it hardly matters. He can't lose her. He lost her years ago.

Cassie sits down beside him at her break. Her eyes look red & puffy. *Did you ever hit her?* she asks. *Did you beat her up?*

Oh God. Of course not. I never touched her. I wouldn't go near her when she made me mad. I was scared to.

But you wanted to? Right? You wanted to hurt your own wife?

No. It's not like that. I didn't want to. But she made me mad. I was scared I might.

I don't understand you at all.

Jesus. I didn't want to ever tell you... but maybe I'll have to. He stares out the window a while, then finally talks. *When I was a kid my dad used to shove my mother around. Sometimes she had black eyes. I wanted to stop him, but couldn't. I was just a runty little kid. He'd go away after it happened, be gone for months, but then he always showed up again. The last time he broke her arm. The hospital called the cops & he never came back.*

Grandpa?

Yeah. But it only happened when he'd been drinking. He was good to us the rest of the time.

Cassie is squeezing her eyes shut as though she can't bear to see him.

David shudders; he regrets saying anything. *Oh God*, he says, *I shouldn't have told you. It's not fair. I shouldn't tell terrible stories about him. Especially now, when he can't defend himself. I feel like I've betrayed him.* Is she even listening to him? David can't tell, but keeps talking anyway. *He hasn't touched a drop for years, though. He finally signed himself into a clinic & they helped him stop.*

Those days were so long ago, in a different lifetime. The gentle helpless old man: Cassie loves him; David suddenly realizes he loves him too. There's no way to reach him & tell him; anyway his father has forgotten everything, the good years & the bad. Maybe it's just as well.

But you never hit Mom?

No. But I was scared I might be like him. I didn't want to be. I was scared that I might have inherited it somehow.

Like blue eyes?

Sounds crazy, doesn't it? But yes, I guess so. Like blue eyes. I don't think so any more. In fact, I think it's just the opposite. I've never hurt anyone in my life. I couldn't swat you when you were little. Even when you deserved it. Your mother would slap your hand if you were doing something dangerous, & she'd tease me because I couldn't.

David looks straight at Cassie. *We were happy then. I want to be sure you know that. We used to be happy. We started drifting apart somehow. Maybe everyone does. So we'd have a drink or two every evening. It made it easier to talk. Your mother started drinking during the day. It was harder for her. She was alone more. I guess she was just drinking because she was unhappy, but she seemed to turn into a different person. I can't tell you why it all happened. I've never figured it out. If I knew I'd tell you.*

There. He's told her. He hopes she's happy. But of course not. How could she be? He's not either. He squeezes her hand & starts to leave.

Just a sec. Cassie runs after him out the door, hugs him quick, then runs back in.

Wow! he thinks, a breakthrough.

She must have regretted it. The next time he enters Civilizations she doesn't speak.

SUSAN

Susan reads everything she can find on squirrels.

Someone spent a winter studying squirrels from a kitchen window:

> *...By spring...I had made 782 notations. I had observed 571 squirrels mostly in the middle of the day when the temperature was warmest...*
>
> *...they chased each other five times as often in February, the mating season, as in April...*

Susan has wasted so much time looking out her bedroom window; she could have studied her own squirrels & made notes.

She keeps on reading:

> *...By noting which branches the squirrels used in crossing from one side of the yard to the other, I identified their aerial highway...*

Susan is amazed. She watched squirrels in the trees, but not scientifically, never noticed whether they followed one series of branches more than another, whether they chased each other more often during certain months. She wasted so much time. She tries to make up for lost time now, & searches for more information.

> *...The grey squirrel moults twice each year...All his fur is replaced in the spring moult, which commences at his head; the autumn moult moves in the opposite direction, and excludes his tail...*

How much else in life has she been missing?

After she finishes her novel she will study squirrels on weekends. She could collect her observations in a book. Or she could include other animals, birds, insects, whatever she sees in her garden. Other people would read her book & be amazed & begin to look around carefully too. City people, leading the same kind of ordinary life as she does, having only weekends to pay close attention, will read her book & be inspired.

Susan has a sudden glimpse of how lives go on, building on the ones that preceded them, lives that don't necessarily depend on children in order to do this.

CASSIE

Michael is the boy that Cassie has been waiting for all through high school, the boy she has been dreaming of, saving her virginity for. He's the reason she ignored all the boys who asked her out. She knew this, as soon as she saw him.

He doesn't look like she'd imagined. He's an ordinary person, not a prince in some fairy tale or movie.

It's hard to know what Michael's thinking. He still calls her by the names of different castles. He seems to watch her; she can't be sure, because she doesn't want to look straight at him. If she pays attention & he's not interested, it will be awful. Everyone will notice. She'd quit her job rather than face them. She'd rather miss a chance with Michael than risk humiliation. It is safer to ignore him.

Perhaps he secretly yearns to get to know her. Perhaps he dreams of her at night. Perhaps he is the person who phones & hangs up when she answers. Too bad for Michael if this is true. He will have to make the first move, & the second & the third. Cassie won't give him any encouragement. This way, if he pursues her, she will know he really wants to.

Meanwhile, the other girls at work think Michael's cute. They giggle when he's around, & talk about him when he's not. They ask, *Don't you think he's gorgeous?* Cassie says she's never noticed.

One of them mentions that she plans to ask him out. Cassie doesn't want this to happen; Michael might say yes.

I heard he has a girlfriend. Cassie hears herself confide this, as though she tells the girl for her own good. The girl thanks her, is happy to be saved from embarrassment. She tells the others what a nice kid Cassie is.

Cassie is everyone's friend. Except Michael's. Anyway, she ignores him.

SUSAN

Susan thinks about her husband's death. Wondering about suicide made it seem almost true.

She keeps thinking unreasonable thoughts that shock her:

He might have mentioned his intention before I bought so many groceries. Before I bought a pot roast, for heaven's sake. Angela & I don't even like pot roast.

Cassie is strong. She must take after someone. Not her mother. Maybe her dead father. Especially if he planned the car crash that killed him. If he killed himself rather than die from cancer, he was stronger than anyone ever imagined.

CASSIE & DAVID

How come you never married again? Cassie asks David.

I don't know. I just never met anyone else. I didn't look. Too scared maybe. He shrugs. *Anyway I don't have time. I'm at the nursing home every evening. I don't meet many people.*

It's good, what you're doing for Grandpa.

Well, I want to see him while I can. It's not because I have to. I just want to. We missed out on so many years.

She is silent. Then, *Did you ever talk to him about it? You know, him hitting your mother.*

No. I kept putting it off. I wasn't sure I could handle it. I guess I waited too long. By the time I got up my nerve it was too late. He didn't even know who I was. Maybe it's just as well.

You go there anyway though. Even though he hit your mother. I don't understand it. He doesn't even know you. It doesn't make sense.

Maybe it's become a habit. As he says it, he realizes it's true. Damn. Something he didn't want to know.

What was she like?

Who?

Your mother. My other grandma.

Oh, how can I tell you what she was like? She was pretty special. You were just a baby when she died. But she'd have spoiled you. You were her only grandchild & she was so proud. She'd push you around the park in your carriage. She was just a little bit of a thing, maybe five feet high, but you should have seen her shoving that carriage along, with her head tossed high in the sky, strutting like a peacock. If she hadn't died she'd have spoiled you rotten.

I wish I'd known her.

I'll bring you a picture.

SUSAN

Susan is reading a library book in Civilizations.

The word squirrel comes from the Latin sciurus or sciurolus, which came from the Greek, — skia, meaning shade, & oura, meaning tail: a creature in the shadow of its tail. A lovely description, she thinks, & considers squirrel tails.

If their tails weren't bushy, squirrels would look like rats: rats scurry up & down the oak trees, chase each other across her roof, run toward her on the lawn, then stop suddenly & dart away. It is not a friendly frisky picture.

This must be an example of Darwinian development, she thinks: a rodent develops a bushy tail, which makes it seem so cute that humans never consider traps & poison. Susan had assumed the tail was for balance, to perform dazzling acrobatics on branches & telephone wires, & jump from one roof to another. Now she thinks the whole thing is pretence. The squirrel wears a bushy tail so people will love it, & they do. Even now Susan thinks they're cute, while she wonders how many chew the wiring in her house.

This is not getting her novel written.

Every day Cassie's mother goes to work & copes, is even successful. It amazes Cassie. Sometimes she's with her mother & meets ex-students. They tell Cassie she's so lucky. Her mother's their favourite teacher. She's the reason they like books, & might teach English some day themselves.

Cassie doesn't know what they're talking about.

Perhaps her mother learned to teach when she was still young & brave & capable, then practised & practised, until the whole thing became a habit.

SUSAN

The man Susan watches is not remarkable at all. She can't imagine why he interests her. He looks like anyone, but on the other hand, she could recognize him a block away by the way he walks. Quick, decisive. He talks the same way. If he comes face to face with her & has to speak, he says hello brusquely, gets it over with as quickly as possible; he is probably flippant, sarcastic. She thinks he must be witty. Occasionally he smiles. It always startles her. His brittle expression suddenly shatters into a thousand shiny pieces with that smile. He smiles as though he hadn't meant to, as though a moment later he regrets it. Susan tries to think of some way to see that smile again.

She has never seen him laugh.

He speaks when he sees her & she answers back. Or sometimes she speaks first, but what can she possibly say? *Hi. Nice day. Haven't seen you around for a while.* She'll have to think up better opening lines to see that smile again.

One day she's in the line-up behind him waiting for a coffee refill. *Hey*, she says, *don't take it all. Save some for me.*

He tells her, *Forget it. This is mine. You've had enough.*

You're not exactly gallant, Susan says, & he agrees, *That's right. I'm not.*

Susan laughs, but when she tells Angela about it later, it doesn't sound funny.

Angela is happy about the trapping though. Now that the

noises are being taken care of, she & Susan find things to talk about over supper.

How are your grandparents? Susan asks. *I haven't seen them for ages. I should drop in some time.*

Did they know about his cancer? Susan wonders. She can't ask them. Perhaps they wonder whether she knows & are afraid to ask her too.

CASSIE

Today when Michael sees Cassie, he calls her Glamis Castle & tells her how to spell it. *But it's pronounced glahms, he says. It's where the queen mother grew up. Somewhere in Scotland.*

Cassie thinks about the queen mother. She is terribly old, even older than Cassie's grandmother. Her little princesses were born before the second war. Cassie has seen pictures from that war: the queen wearing a blue dress & a string of pearls, the king looking serious, two little girls in matching coats & hats. Now those children are older than Cassie's parents. She tries to imagine the queen mother growing up in a Scottish castle, tries to imagine her ever being a young girl at all.

She has blue eyes, says Michael. Like you. Her eyes are famous.

Cassie can't believe Michael ever looked straight at her & saw her eyes. Someone else at Civilizations must have mentioned their colour to him.

She wonders what colour his eyes are, & can't imagine how to find out.

SUSAN

There are more squirrels in Susan's house than the trapper expected. In the small space between the bedroom ceiling & the roof, squirrels still fuck, pee, defecate, chase back & forth. All this activity makes them hungry. When they run out of acorns they will chew on wiring. Susan lies awake at night & imagines she hears them munch.

They will burn the house down around her.

People keep telling her squirrel stories. The mailman has squirrels in his front verandah, fierce ones that chase his cat. He uses the side door to avoid them. *Be glad yours aren't aggressive,* he tells her.

Be glad yours stay outside, she answers. *At least you're safe once you get in.*

In Susan's nightmares, squirrels clutch at Angela with their non-retractable claws, they bite with sharp incisors. She wakes up shaking. Susan has never heard of squirrels attacking people. It doesn't matter. It still happens inside her dreams.

Susan & Angela switch bedrooms. After all, Susan is the mother; this seems like the maternal thing to do. She wonders why she hadn't done it earlier.

She keeps decreasing her dose of valium, chops bits off each half-tablet with a bread knife. Enough is enough.

She lies awake in Angela's bedroom & remembers a line from Ibsen's *A Doll's House*:

... When did my squirrel come home?...

As if it would be possible not to hear them arrive. A crash somewhere to the left above her head, then rustling, a scurry.

As if they don't make their presence felt. Invisible. But all around her. Like religion, or concepts of God & Satan. Perhaps some day Susan will believe in them again. Right now she only believes in squirrels.

She thinks of atoms, microbes. Galileo or Leeuwenhoek or someone peered through the first microscope & saw the invisible. He must have thought he'd discovered God, or that God was waiting to be discovered next, sprawled out on a petri dish to be stained, magnified, analyzed.

SUSAN

The oak trees are the reason Susan moved into this house. From a second storey window she sees them begin to branch. The trunks split vertically into huge limbs which stretch high into the sky. They pull Susan's eyes up there with them. When people visit, she shows them the oak trees from her back window & expects her guests to admire them. Even late at night; darkness is no excuse.

She might tell them that fossils of tree squirrels date back 28 million years, to the Lower Miocene period. Or she might not.

But the squirrels were here first, not just in Genesis, but in her city neighbourhood. She likes to think about this. The oak trees were here, & squirrels lived inside them. They built enormous leaf nests, high up in the forks of the trees. They knew how to do this, made a base using small branches that had leaves fastened on, then lined it with leaves, grasses, shredded bark. But the squirrels in Susan's neighbourhood don't need to do this any longer. They made another Darwinian adaptation & moved into Susan's house.

Susan remembers moving into this house herself; was it only a few months ago? Squirrels were everywhere, on the lawn, on the sidewalk, on hydro wires, always moving. Running, climbing, leaping from branch to branch, chasing each other up & down tree trunks, rustling through the oak leaves high above the house.

Susan took them for granted, & never worried whether they had somewhere to spend the night. On rainy days she didn't wonder where they found shelter.

There'd been so many new noises to get used to, like moving in with someone, adjusting to the way a stranger coughs & breathes & chews. This house seemed like an old person, idiosyncratic, set in its ways. It was warm & all the windows were open. They'd hear a noise, & wonder whether it was in their house or a neighbour's. Voices. Creaks. Taps running. Toilets flushing. Music. Hums of refrigerators, air conditioners, fans. Laughter. Hammering. Noises they gradually became used to.

Rustlings. Animals running back & forth above their heads. They wondered why animals loved their roof so much, feeling a bit smug about it. The dilapidated charm of the house had attracted Susan. Maybe the squirrels had some sort of sixth sense & recognized it too.

In the summer Susan felt safely burrowed inside a forest. From her back window she could see a dozen oak trees.

But now it's autumn. Acorns keep falling down, naturally perhaps, or forced loose by squirrel claws. Soon the leaves will be gone. Bare skeletal branches will be silhouetted against the sky, with not a squirrel nest in sight.

Susan reads:

...Female greys have a peculiar mating call, similar to the quacking of a duck, which is used to announce they are in heat. The effect of this call is electric, and it may summon as many as a dozen suitors who chase her through the trees. Initially she spurns them all, but eventually accepts one...

Susan watched them chase through the trees in a mad frenzy. She watched from her bedroom window & presumed they were playing.

She thought this, in the same way she watches small children, & thinks them innocent. Children know what they want, & are direct. *Hold me,* they can say. *Kiss me. Make it better.* Susan is 44 years old, & can't remember being a child.

It is impossible to remember being with her husband.

...Their pairing is brief, and the male leaves her minutes after the event...

It would be so easy if that were all she wanted.

She was married a long time, & knows relationships aren't perfect. She was married 20 years, & spent much of it wondering why.

It is so hard & so easy when men die.

SUSAN

Susan's not good at guessing ages. She watches the man in Civilizations & wonders how old he is.

Age never used to matter; now she looks inside a mirror & can watch herself grow older.

She thinks she hasn't learned much along the way, perhaps because of all those gaps in her memory, in her thinking, in her life. She pretends to be whatever age people tell her; & they are always telling her. The government thinks she's 44 & prints the appropriate year of birth on her driver's license & birth certificate. Bureaucrats make typing errors. Everyone knows this.

Her mother agrees with them, but she is old & forgetful. Susan's brother is wrong too. All through childhood he'd assumed she was older than him; he still thinks this.

If Susan was the age her mother & brother imagine her to be, she would not live in this old house, with its absence of attic, its presence of squirrels. If Susan WAS 44, Angela would have grown up & moved away. Susan would have developed a different life-style. She would live in a condominium, attend the opera & symphony & talk knowledgeably of music at intermissions. She'd cook pesto sauce & pasta primavera, would know one white wine from another. She'd travel to exotic foreign places on her vacations. There's some mistake about her age, but she keeps this to herself. Not like the squirrels in the attic that she mentions to complete strangers.

If Susan ever gets to know the man in Civilizations, or any man, if she ever trusts a man again, when they share personal information, Susan wonders what age she'll say. She can't decide. Perhaps this is one reason she ignores him.

But there are some things she could tell him that are simple & innocuous & don't make an emotional statement or commitment: *A squirrel eats a couple of pounds of food a week.*

Probably because they're so active, the man might say. She'd agree & mention their speed: *They can run 25 kilometres an hour.* Perhaps he'd calculate their food intake in terms of body weight: a squirrel weighing about 450 grams, eating two pounds of food a week... They'd scribble on paper serviettes, trying to figure out how much food, relatively speaking, that would be for an average man weighing 170 pounds.

Or:

There aren't any black squirrels in the southern states, only grey ones. So scientists think the squirrel gene for black colouring is associated with adaptation to cold weather.

He would listen & be amazed. He'd never heard this before. It might turn out he has an interest in genetics. Perhaps he would tell stories of his own & amaze her.

Or:

Squirrel tracks in the snow look like exclamation marks!!

She could tell him about squirrels. He could tell her who he is.

Or:

Because the squirrel was so small & active, early American settlers became crack shots. People speculate this helped them defeat the British during the American Revolution.

Ernest Thompson Seton wrote about this, she might add, so he'll believe her, because this is the kind of true story that sounds ridiculous.

She could tell him these things to break the ice. Once she gets to trust him, she will tell him all her secrets. Later, when she has figured out what they are.

There are things that she tells no one.

Cassie's father had cancer.

Long after he died, Cassie's mother finds out. The family doctor mentions it casually, assuming she already knew.

Cassie's father knew he had it. He lived with the knowledge somehow, but never told his wife.

Cancer. Cassie's mother hears that word from the doctor & realizes she never knew her husband. He kept that enormous secret from her. What other things had he never told her?

He sends her a bulletin from the grave: *I never needed you at all.*

She thinks he must have confided in somebody. Surely someone gave him comfort. She wonders who it was, though it hardly matters now. But she has saved all his papers so Cassie could have them some day. Maybe she should look through them & remove whatever Cassie shouldn't see.

But what shouldn't she see? If her father had a lover Cassie should know it. Perhaps she'd want to meet her. They could talk together & cry about the man that they both loved.

Because Cassie's mother won't talk about him. Not yet. Not until she forgives him. He faced cancer without her comfort. She can't accept this.

His death; the car accident that never made sense, losing control while driving alone near an embankment. He was always a careful driver.

Now Cassie's mother wonders about that accident.

Was he distracted? Thinking of cancer. Wondering how his wife & daughter would get along without him.

Suicide. Cassie's mother refuses to say the word aloud in case it begins to seem like a possibility.

Cancer. She doesn't like to say that word either. Some day soon she'll tell Cassie about the cancer. Or maybe not.

Until that moment in the doctor's office Cassie's mother wanted to stay in familiar surroundings with comfortable old memories all around her. Suddenly she sold the house & moved away.

Cassie's mother is getting stronger. She looks inside the mirror & sees herself grow old but also strong.

SUSAN

Every couple of days another squirrel is caught in a trap. When they hear the door bang shut, Susan & Angela go outside & look straight up. Far above them an angry squirrel bangs against the side, tries to get out. Susan leaves a message on the trapper's answering machine. She dials slowly, sadly, aware that she is interfering with something that should be left to chance. She wonders whether he takes each squirrel to the same place so they can find each other again, whether it matters anyway, whether they have any chance of survival, being dumped in autumn in a strange area where other squirrels have already established territories. She wonders whether he thinks to check for oak trees.

She keeps hearing noises. Squirrels still live above her head.

Perhaps the squirrels the trapper hauls away are not from Susan's attic at all. Squirrels from neighbouring houses may be attracted to her roof by the smell of peanut butter.

Every few days the trapper removes a squirrel, & puts an empty cage on the roof. *That's seven of them gone now*, he tells her.

Maybe they keep returning, Susan says. *Maybe you trap the same ones over & over.*

No way, he says. *I'd recognize them if they came back. Anyway I take them too far away. Listen lady, I don't want to re-trap them. It's no picnic, climbing around up on your roof. I don't get extra money per squirrel. You're just paying me by the job.*

He's so sure they won't come back that it makes her wonder. *I don't see how you can be so certain...* She hesitates.

He knows what she's thinking. *I don't kill them, if that's what you mean.*

She thinks of what it means to kill squirrels, to kill anything, & remembers an old poem she memorized when she was young:

> *Like a small grey*
> *coffee-pot,*
> *sits the squirrel.*
> *He is not*
>
> *all he should be,*
> *kills by dozens*
> *trees, and eats*
> *his red-brown cousins.*
>
> *The keeper on the*
> *other hand,*
> *who shot him, is*
> *a Christian, and*
>
> *loves his enemies,*
> *which shows*
> *the squirrel was not*
> *one of those.*

SUSAN

One day Susan is home with the flu when the trapper arrives. She watches from a dark window.

She hears noises, voices, the ladder being unfastened from his truck, carried down between the houses, bumping against the fence, being set into place in her neighbour's back yard. She hears him talk to someone, the clang of his boots on each rung of the metal ladder. He passes her window, grabbing the ladder with one hand, carrying an empty cage in the other. She hears him shinny up the roof, slipping back a little, then scrambling up again.

He calls to someone on the ground who hollers back. After a few minutes she hears him sliding down the roof. She looks down, expecting to see him on the ground, his limbs splayed out at awkward angles, not moving. He's not there. Somehow, he must have come to a stop at the edge of the roof. A stranger stands in the backyard next door, shading his eyes, looking at the roof somewhere above her window. She hears sounds over her head, then the trapper's foot on a rung of the ladder. He passes by her window again on the way back down. He is carrying a cage; a black squirrel thrashes inside it. Susan realizes she has been holding her breath.

She leaves a message on his answering machine: *It's not worth getting hurt over.*

He calls her back & laughs. Susan wonders whether he'd known she was watching & dramatized the climb.

He says, *I'm not planning to get hurt. Don't worry. I know what I'm doing.*

She hopes so.

SUSAN

Susan's story isn't going well. It seems to be over. She has nothing else she wants to write.

Maybe she needs more characters. Susan thinks about the man in the restaurant & wonders how to write him into the story. Also Michael. He & the real Cassie are obviously attracted to each other. Some problem should thwart their romance for a while, then later be resolved. Susan tramps through the park & tries to think of ways to do this.

It's fall, & acorns are falling from oak trees. They fall all around her, thud on the grass, clunk on the asphalt path. It is breezy; perhaps that explains it. But Susan begins to think the acorns aren't falling at random; they're being aimed right at her. She's determined not to let it spook her, & continues walking under the oaks, slowly, to make an easy target.

Afterward she goes to Civilizations for coffee. Perhaps she looks dishevelled, because the cashier asks whether she's all right.

It's the squirrels, Susan says, then tells about the trapper removing them from her attic. *All this worry about squirrels must have spooked me. In the park just now I'd have sworn they were throwing acorns at me.*

You're joking, right? says Cassie.

I wouldn't kid about something this important, Susan tells her. *Anyway, those squirrels are lousy shots. I played softball when I was your age. My aim's a lot better than theirs.* Susan's finally laughing. *If they ever hit me with an acorn they'd better watch out. I'll throw it back.*

CASSIE

Cassie watches the woman writing in her notebook. Is she okay? All that talk about squirrels throwing acorns at her... it sounded crazy. But the woman seemed to be serious. Just thinking about it gives Cassie the creeps.

Usually the woman sits quietly in her corner & watches everyone & writes. Today she just sits there, the notebook closed, no pen in sight.

Cassie wants to offer her a pencil & remind her to get to work.

DAVID

David resents his father's illness; Alzheimer's Disease is so unfair. It takes so much away from his father, of course, but it also removes from David an aspect of his life, a richness, a history. The loss diminishes David, leaves him rootless. His father's illness is progressive & so is the effect on David. He feels emptier & emptier inside.

Each time David visits he hopes for a lucid moment. He waits for his father to recognize him & say, *There is something I always meant to tell you,* & then tell David what it is.

Whatever it is will be important, will give deeper meaning to David's life. This is the dream that keeps him going.

People at work think he's unselfish, a model son. David is uncomfortable with their perception, but there's no way he'll admit the truth: he visits his father because he needs to.

DAVID

It is Saturday. David has been to Civilizations earlier in the day. He's at home alone in his high-rise apartment when it happens.

Suddenly the world doesn't seem solid. It doesn't hold David up the way it used to. Something is happening inside him. It starts inside his head & then shudders right through his body. He grabs a table for support. He falls toward an armchair.

He sits still, afraid to move. He listens to himself breathe & wonders what is going on inside him. Is this how a stroke happens? The way a heart shivers before it stops? He feels his pulse to make sure he's still alive.

Perhaps only a few minutes go by. He has not been pondering earth-time. Finally he thinks the spell, whatever it was, is passing. Or maybe he is. Perhaps this is the way people die. Initial panic, & then a peaceful moment before the end.

Cassie. He will die before she forgives him.

His father. Who will care for him when David dies?

Sons don't die before their fathers. Not healthy ones. Suddenly he regrets his aversion to jogging, his passion for carrot cake with vanilla icing. But these vices seemed unimportant, not serious enough to kill him.

Give me another chance, he hears someone say. It seems to be his voice.

He isn't ready. He has a daughter who doesn't like him. There are things he has to tell her; he doesn't even know what they are yet. He has a father who waits to be fed.

On the other hand, he still seems to be alive. He feels euphoric as he realizes this.

David focuses on the face of his watch. Five o'clock. Daylight.

He tries to remember why he's home. Surely he ought to be somewhere between his office & the nursing home right now. The supper trays will be arriving.

He looks around his apartment, searching for a clue. He's not wearing office clothes. It must be the weekend. He checks the newspaper. Saturday. Yes. Of course.

David tries to get up from his chair & discovers he can manage it. He feels a little shaky, but otherwise all right. The spell, whatever it was, seems to be over. Both hands move. Both arms. Both legs.

He tries to dial the nursing home; he can do this.

He wonders whether he'll be able to talk. He pictures one side of his face without expression, drool forming at the side of his mouth, his tongue uncontrollable, his throat unable to make sounds that people can understand. Ejaculations of spit spurting into the telephone receiver. The nurse's voice, *Yes. Hello? Who is this?*, then becoming impatient, thinking it's some kind of crank call, a heavy breather.

3-G, the nurse says, & David is able to talk. He hears himself explain who he is, that he'll be late, could they please feed his father. The nurse understands him. He feels weak in his knees again, this time from relief. He hasn't been stricken inarticulate, isn't helpless like his father. He feels tears forming inside his eyes.

Don't worry, the nurse is saying, *Take your time, or, better yet, take a night off. We'll feed your father & get him walking. I'll tell him the buses are delayed because of the earthquake.*

Earthquake?

Sure. Didn't you feel it? You must be the only one in the city who didn't. Even the staff was scared. Anyway, things have finally calmed down here.

An earthquake. Of course. He should have realized.

It's Saturday night, she says. *Take the night off. Go out & have some fun.*

So he's not going to die after all. Not yet. Unless he is careless & walks in front of a speeding car. A bank robber could fire a random shot into a crowd. A rabid animal could attack him. Life is uncertain; it always has been.

He has a night off. He should use it.

Civilizations closes at eight o'clock. Does Cassie get off then? Does she stay late & help clean up? He has no idea. She probably goes out later with her friends, whoever her friends are. She must have some. He ought to know them.

He can go there & eat supper. She will either be there or she won't. She will speak or she'll ignore him. Perhaps she'll take a coffee break & sit & chat while he is eating, or ask him to wait around so they can go for a walk when she gets off work. Perhaps he will be brave enough to suggest it himself.

Sometimes he & Cassie reach for words & find them. It's becoming easier. Lately sometimes they talk.

SUSAN & CASSIE & MICHAEL

Now when Cassie sees Susan she thinks of acorns. *Have you been back to the park?* Cassie asks.

No. Trying to get my courage up, I guess. But a lot of acorns fell today during that tremor. They sounded like bullets hitting the roof. My street is covered with acorns now. It's like walking on ball bearings. Anyway they'll disappear soon. The squirrels will take them.

Michael comes up behind them, says, *Yeah. They'll be squirrelling them away.* Susan & Cassie laugh.

I think they're cute, Cassie says. *My grandmother has a powder puff on her dresser. Squirrel tails remind me of it.*

People used to use squirrel tails to make fishing lures, says Michael. *I read it somewhere.*

Down south they eat squirrel pie, Susan tells them. *They think it's a delicacy.*

Michael makes a face. *Yuck!*

You should tell Michael your enchanted forest story, says Cassie.

So Susan tells him about walking beneath the oak trees, daring gods or squirrels or oak trees to hit her with acorns. She laughs, knowing it sounds crazy. *There were cars parked all along the street beside the park,* Susan says. *The acorns made a terrible racket as they crashed onto those cars. I expected the hoods to be dented. It's windy this evening. Maybe I'll go back there to see what happens.*

Michael is fascinated. *We'll be off work soon,* he says. *Maybe Cassie & I can go with you.*

Great. The more of us the better. It'll be harder for the squirrels to miss us all.

Michael & Cassie. Susan wonders how can she bear to be with them. She's trying to forget she was ever that young.

When Susan buys a refill of coffee she asks Cassie, *How do you like working here anyway?* She needs to know so she can write down the answer in her notebook. If someone ever asks the Cassie in her story, Susan will have an answer handy.

So, you're going to show us your squirrels tonight. Both of us, Michael & me, Cassie says. *That's great, really great,* she adds, looking more animated than usual.

The restaurant is crowded. Susan's papers are spread out all over the table to discourage strangers from sitting down with her. It's just as well.

The man comes into Civilizations. Susan knows this, even though they don't make eye contact.

DAVID & CASSIE

The restaurant is always crowded. David can never understand it. Who are all these people? They go out for supper as though it's nothing, as though they are entitled & deserve to. They seem to belong here; they eat a quiche & salad or soup & coffee; they chat with friends.

Cassie doesn't see him until he's in front of the cash register, fumbling with his wallet.

Dad!

Hi Honey.

How come you're here? You came this morning.

Well, I decided to come back.

Grandpa. Is he all right? Why aren't you there?

He's okay. I keep forgetting that nurses work there. They'll take care of him. I took the night off & thought maybe you might be free.

Well...

Grandpa won't know whether I'm there or not. I can't put off getting to know my daughter until after my father dies. As David hears himself say it, he knows it's true. He sees Cassie every weekend, & is beginning to find the words that have to be said. He can't risk losing her again. If it's even possible to reach her. If it's not already too late.

Cassie stares at him.

He misunderstands. *I won't neglect him. I'll drop in sometimes on my lunch hour. I just won't go there every single night. Maybe alternate ones.*

David sees that Cassie looks stricken. Probably she thinks she'll be responsible for him every second night, the same way he takes care of his father.

He tries to reassure her. *I need some time for myself. Maybe I'll take a course at night school. Do things.*

She is silent, & he has no idea what she's thinking. *Maybe I should have phoned you first...*

No. It's okay. Hang around. We can talk later.

DAVID & MICHAEL

David sits & watches people, the way they eat. He's so used to watching his father & the other old men. The people in this restaurant seem so young. He watches their expressions as they talk, the different ways they chew their food. Some of them sit alone; they read books, fill in crossword puzzles.

His daughter at the cash desk looks like her mother did at her age. It's not her fault.

She's talking to a busboy. They look at him & smile; David feels himself smile back.

David's startled when the busboy comes over to his table & speaks, *Um. I've been wondering something.*

David waits.

How come you named your daughter Cassie? the boy asks.

David laughs. The question is so unexpected. *I can't remember*, he says, then adds, *But anyway, why not?*

The boy laughs as though David has said something terribly funny. David smiles. Maybe he has.

David hopes Cassie noticed that he made the busboy laugh, that the busboy seems to like him, or at least doesn't hate him. Perhaps this has been some kind of a test.

Did you feel the tremor earlier? David asks him, still looking for reassurance that an earthquake really happened.

SUSAN

Susan notices the man speak to Cassie. She tries to seem busy writing in her notebook as he passes with his coffee, goes back for cream or sugar, then returns to his seat. She senses that he hesitates beside her table before moving on.

If she looked up he would speak, & she would. What would they say? This is what she always wonders. Would she be able to make conversation? If she did speak, she'd say too much. She tends to babble when she's nervous.

She'd be likely to tell him everything, whatever that is: her life history, family stories about her mother & brother who think she's older, her dead husband & his snapshots, her daughter who abandons her each weekend, the squirrels above the bedroom ceiling, the peanut butter inside the traps, how she is responsible for the squirrels being trapped & taken away, whatever that means, whatever the implications are. *Events have gotten out of hand,* she would tell him, *like writing a story, the way characters take over & do whatever they want.*

Then she might tell him about her novel, how she would like to write him into it, but doesn't know enough about him, would have to make things up. This would be his signal to talk about himself, to tell her too much, more than she can listen to at once, more than she is ready to know.

Susan doesn't want this. She wants their relationship to develop slowly, by inches; centimetres would be even better.

She wants to discover him a little more each day. A couple of years into the future she wouldn't be bored; he wouldn't either. They'd still be discovering more jigsaw puzzle pieces of each other, studying them, turning them this way & that, fitting them perfectly into place.

In another couple of months she'll be ready to have coffee with him.

So Susan doesn't look up. It's too risky. She tries to concentrate on her story.

Later she's aware that he gets up again & speaks to Cassie. Susan writes this in her notebook.

When he returns someone has taken his table. There are no empty ones left.

Mind if I join you? he asks someone else. Susan wants to scream or weep.

Sure. No problem, the woman says, & begins a conversation. She seems to know how to do this. The man answers because he is polite.

Susan knows he wishes the woman would leave him alone, so he can secretly watch Susan. He wears tinted glasses; it would be easy.

Susan ignores him & writes her story.

It is time to tell Cassie about her father's cancer. Cassie can handle it, of course, & her mother is now strong enough to tell her.

It is time to put these things behind her.

DAVID

David practises how to talk to Cassie after work. Perhaps he will be able to explain to her how it was. *We were so young when we got married,* he'll tell her. *Not much older than you are. We made mistakes. You know how it is when you're insecure. You're afraid to admit you're wrong. That's how we both were.*

That's how he still is.

He could tell her more: *We thought your mother was pregnant. Her period was late. We had no choice. Kids didn't have options in those days. A minister married us in his vestry. Just our parents present. Both mothers crying. My father heard about it somehow & showed up. The fathers glaring at each other. Each one blamed the other for not bringing his kid up right. We had a one-night honeymoon at a hotel downtown. It was all we could afford. By the next morning your mother had her period. If we'd known some way to untie the knot we would have. It still seems like a bad joke.*

He could tell her, but he won't.

& he won't tell how ignorant they were. The first time they tried to have intercourse, she asked, *Did you get it out in time?* Him embarrassed, almost laughing, *I didn't even get it in yet.* They were so innocent. He feels like crying when he remembers how young they were.

You didn't communicate, is the way Cassie will probably put it, & she'll be right. Probably she'll spout some bits of Freud. She is young & was hurt & is entitled.

It isn't fair, she'll say. She always says this. He'll have to agree. *Life ISN'T fair,* he'll tell her. *Life isn't perfect. But it's better than the alternative.* That old cliché. Then they'll think about his father who's slowly dying.

How's your grandma? he'll ask her. *Does she make you eat senna leaves each morning? Did I ever tell you about my grandmother who made me eat them?*

Or they'll walk & talk about nothing, about school, about the weather, her job at Civilizations, the busboy who asked about her name.

In time the words that matter will be said. Words, the ones he doesn't know yet, or can't express. Sooner or later he'll figure them out. Probably not tonight, but sometime.

IF I KNEW I'D TELL YOU

CASSIE & DAVID

After work Cassie tells David, *One of the customers always talks about squirrels. She claims squirrels throw acorns at her in the park. She really seems to believe this. After work Michael & I had arranged to go there with her to see if anything happens. They're outside waiting for us. Do you want to go or not?*

Michael? The boy who spoke to me earlier?

Yeah. It's sort of silly. They're going anyway, but we don't have to. What do you think?

Of course I want to go, David says. *Squirrels have always ignored me. They've never thrown acorns in my direction. I'm not getting any younger. It's time they started.*

Okay. Come on then. They're waiting.

He sees them. It's the woman who watches people & writes things down.

137

SUSAN & MICHAEL

Susan waits with Michael. Cassie is inviting the man to join them. There must be some good reason why she does this.

Would it be okay? she'd asked Susan first.

Of course. Why not? What else could she say? Why couldn't it be anyone else?

This man. This man Susan dreams of, who touches her inside her dreams. Dreaming is enough. It's all she wants. She can get along without him, or anyone. She can try to write her novel. She can live inside her house, can buy baseboard & quarter-round if she wants to, & can saw it into pieces. She can buy a mitre-box in order to do this really well. When she nails the wood in place it will be as final as the hiring of a trapper, as hammering nails in a husband's coffin. Something will finally be dealt with, & be over.

She can write notes to Angela on self-stick paper, & read the ones Angela writes to her. Perhaps their notes & conversations will be enough, until some day Angela moves away.

Perhaps she can get to know Angela again. Once she thought she knew her. Other people's lives, Susan thinks, you think you know them but you don't. It's fair though, because other people don't know you either.

She can haunt libraries, & hunt up bits of information to make small talk with men in restaurants. If she wants to risk it. If she wants to watch a man, & daydream, & wonder whether he watches her when she's not looking.

She can ignore men. It is possible to be alone. She has memorized 'The Love Song of J. Alfred Prufrock,' & knows it can be done.

She can hide in Civilizations & write down anything she wants.

I hope those squirrels are still around, Michael says.

Susan had forgotten all about him. She remembers a poem by Raymond Souster & recites it to Michael:

> *Our world an acorn*
> *in the teeth of a squirrel.*
> *We wait and we wait*
> *for him to nibble through.*

She can go home & re-read books of poems.
Cassie & the man are coming toward them.

SUSAN & DAVID

We're going to an enchanted forest, Susan tells the man. *Don't come unless you're feeling brave. It'll be scary. Squirrels will throw acorns at your head.*

David thinks she must be crazy. It doesn't matter. He's coming anyway. It'll make his daughter happy.

Susan imagines: They saunter, Cassie & Michael, she & this man, whoever he is, whatever his name is, enjoying the late November twilight. *I know lots of squirrel stories*, she might tell him. He'll pretend he's always wanted to hear some. Or perhaps he'll really mean it.

Arm in arm they'll saunter toward the park.

No. Not arm in arm.

Know any stories about squirrels? Susan asks.

You mean jokes? Like elephant jokes?

No. Just stories. True ones.

He thinks about it. *About squirrels? I guess not.*

That's okay. I know lots.

So, what are you waiting for? I want to hear some.

Perhaps she'll tell him. Perhaps she won't.

This is one way it could happen.

DAVID

David imagines how they look.

They walk toward the park. David sees them as though from a great distance. People watching must imagine that they are couples; he & this woman probably look like the parents of one of the kids.

He wants to stop passers-by & correct them. *It's not what you think. I don't even know this woman's name. But it's my night off, & I can listen to some stranger prattle about squirrels if I want to. I'll be polite. It might win me some points with my daughter.*

They walk into the evening sky, like the end of a Charlie Chaplin movie. But it's not perfect. No fairy-tale ending. But maybe, for Cassie & him, it's some kind of a beginning.

He remembers Chaplin's little tramp, how he walks jerkily away from the camera, then suddenly kicks one foot backward in a bit of a dance. Showing the world that he's not beaten. Not yet.

That little kick, perhaps he'll try it. Probably not. They'd think he was crazy too.

SUSAN

Susan doesn't want to tell this man her secrets after all. But she can tell stories about squirrels to anyone; what does it matter.

Perhaps she'll tell them that squirrels helped win the American Revolution, or mention their preference for Squirrel peanut butter. They'll all laugh. Other people will look at them & smile & think they're happy.

Maybe she IS happy. Maybe she is happier living alone with Angela than when her husband was alive. She can no longer remember how it was before.

She can talk to Cassie & Michael, & ignore the man, the way she does in Civilizations. She can do it easily. She's had practice.

Susan can do this. She can do whatever she wants to. Deciding is the hard part.

ACKNOWLEDGEMENTS

Prologue: From *Being Alive,* by Al Purdy. Used by permission of the Canadian Publishers, McClelland & Stewart, Toronto.

Page 24: Reprinted from *The Complete Works of Saki*, by H.H. Munro, Doubleday, 1976.

Page 35: Reprinted from *The Waste Land*, by T.S. Eliot, Faber and Faber

Page 52: Reprinted from "Here Comes Spring— and 624,000 Raccoons," by Paul King, couresty The Toronto Star Syndicate

Page 94: Reprinted from *Mammals of North America*, by Anne Innis Dagg, Otter Press, 1974, by permission of the author

Page 95, 109, 110: Reprinted from *The Squirrels of Canada*, by S.E. Woods, Jr. Reproduced with the permission of the Canadian Museum of Nature, Ottawa, Canada

Page 107: Reprinted from *A Doll's House*, by Henrik Ibsen, Random House Inc.

Page 116: "The Grey Squirrel," by Humbert Wolfe, is reprinted from *The Penguin Book of Animal Verse*, ed. George McBeth, Penguin Books, 1965

Page 137: "The Acorn" is reprinted from *Collected Poems of Raymond Souster*, by permission of Oberon Press